Chasing Texas

By

Jason Watson

CONTENTS

Nothing Left Here

The story begins on a farm in Northeast Alabama near present day Anniston. This is home for Ezequiel "Zeke" McDaniel, son of Scottish immigrants and Confederate soldier recently home from the war. It doesn't take long for Zeke to realize he has no life left in Alabama, the winter is spent scratching and saving money and supplies so the family can make the move out West the next spring. Zeke knows it will be a long, hard winter. Since the war had just ended there was no money anywhere. It was the first week in December of 1865 when Zeke lost four of his farm hands. He knew it was coming; the fall harvest was terrible so there was no money to pay the hands. There was also very little left to put up in storage.

Not long after the four left, a bad winter storm blew through. There was a little snow but there was a lot of sleet rain and ice, not to mention the high winds. At the height of the storm some of the cattle and pigs broke down a part of the fence and some of them began to scatter. One of the hands saw the cows running loose. He hollered at Zeke. Zeke, the other four farmhands, and his two sons ran outside to round them up. They were out there the better part of the night. When it was all over they had lost five head of cattle.

When they got the cattle penned up and quieted down, they turned their attention to Zeke's young son Jake. Zeke said, "You boys get in the house and shuck them britches. Getcha some dry clothes, and tell yer mama I'll be in directly." While the boys ran into the house to get dry and warm, Zeke and the other hands finished putting up the horses and tack. It was cold outside, the kind of cold that seems to pierce clothing and not stop until it has firmly set into the bones. The majority of the rain was gone but everyone was already soaked and there was still an icy sleet blowing in the air. Although the men could not stop shivering, they knew they had to make sure everything was secure around the barn. If the animals got out again they might not have anything to eat the rest of the winter. Once he was sure that the fence would hold and the hands were all right, Zeke went back to the house to dry himself and get a hot bowl of something to eat.

"You boys alright?" asked Zeke.

"Yes sir," the boys answered, but as Jake was answering his father, he sneezed.

His mother Elizabeth said, "He's caught a fever and a case of chills."

There weren't any doctors to speak of. In those days, especially in rural areas, people were their own doctors. Elizabeth kept Jake covered in a warm wool blanket throughout the night with a cool wet rag on his forehead. There really was not much else they could do for the time being. That night the family settled into their warm and more importantly dry beds to get some well-deserved rest.

The next morning around daybreak, Zeke, Elizabeth and the older son Thomas were up and ready for another day of life in the Post-War South. Zeke, Thomas, and the four remaining farmhands cut out a few cows and drove them to market in Anniston. Elizabeth stayed back to take care of the house and young Jake.

"How are you feeling son?" asked Elizabeth.

"I'm alright, Mama," answered Jake. Jake had always had a fiercely independent streak, which was very common in the McDaniel family on both sides. Elizabeth's family was Scots-Irish. Having settled in the Appalachian Country in the late 1700s, they finally made their way to the bottom of the mountain range in Northern Alabama. Jake didn't want his mother to worry too much about him. He was desperately trying to be the man of the house. Even at a young age, he knew the situation the family was in and that his parents had their plates full already.

"Do ya feel like you can get up and move around?" she asked.

"Yes ma'am," Jake replied.

Jake got up out of bed and sat at the table. Elizabeth had some scrambled eggs with a little ham and biscuits left over. Jake took his fork in one hand and rubbed his sleepy eyes with the other. As he took his first bite of eggs, his mother set a glass of milk next to him.

"Try and eat whatcha can, son, but don't overdo it," Elizabeth explained.

Jake ate a couple of bites and had a couple of sips of milk. Other than that he just poked around at his food.

A few minutes later Jake got up and held his stomach. He made a mad dash for the door but didn't quite make it. He threw up all over the floor and front door. As he lay on the floor, his mother rushed over to help him out.

"It's okay, son, don't worry about that. I'll clean it up. Let's get you back in bed," Elizabeth told Jake in that calming motherly voice that all the great ones have.

Besides the embarrassment and the smell wafting through the small cabin, Jake was no worse for the wear. After getting Jake in bed and cleaned up, she turned her attention to the floor and door. Soon she had it all cleaned up as good as new. She went back over to check on Jake.

"Here, son, take a drink of water," she told him. Jake took only a couple of sips. It wasn't long before he was in the floor dry heaving.

There is no more helpless feeling for a mother than knowing she can't help her sick child. She got him back in bed and covered him up. Jake's temperature had shown no signs of letting up and now he couldn't keep any food down. "Mama, it hurts, my stomach and my head hurts, Mama."

"I know they do, son, I know. I wish I could just take it all away but sometimes we just have to suffer through some pain, but I'm here with you. I won't leave you alone," Elizabeth told him.

Jake took his mother's words with mixed reaction. He felt good that she was there by his side, but that didn't do anything for the pain in his belly and forehead.

That evening Zeke and the other son Thomas returned home. They were able to sell eight cows. The problem was the market for pigs, cows or any other livestock had bottomed out.

"How'd y'all do?" asked Elizabeth curiously.

Zeke sighed and sort of rolled his eyes. "They ain't bringin' what they used to . . . they ain't bringin' what they oughta," said Zeke in a very defeated tone.

"Thomas, fix yourself a plate, I got dinner on the stove, and then check on yer brother. I need to talk to yer pa," Elizabeth said.

"Yes ma'am," Thomas replied.

Elizabeth took Zeke by the arm and they walked out into the cold night air. "What are we gonna do?" she asked her husband.

"I don't know," he replied, "I been thinkin', the harvest fell through last fall. Four hands already quit. I don't blame 'em. I damn shore ain't got no money to give 'em! The market is dryin' up around here. We blew everything to hell for the last five years with cannons and rifles," Zeke paused for a minute, looked at the ground, then said in a low hushed voice, "Maybe it's time we picked up and found us a new place to settle down."

Elizabeth didn't say anything at first. She just thought for a minute and then said, "How long you been thinkin' that?"

"I don't know, awhile now I guess," Zeke said, still looking at the ground.

"This is our home, I know 'tain't much, but it's ours. We're better off than a lot of folks in these parts. We actually made enough money to hire hands," Elizabeth said.

"I know that Liz, but those days is over with. That was all before the war. We ain't doin' no better than anyone else from North Carolina to East Texas. We got no money. Them boys ain't big enough to replace eight hired hands. Even if we got this farm up and runnin' the way it ought to be, there still ain't no market to sell to."

Elizabeth knew everything her husband said was true. She knew it in her heart but she just wasn't ready to admit it with her lips. Knowing that nothing was going to get settled that night in the cold night air, they went back into the house and sat down to a hot meal then off to bed.

A week went by and nothing had improved. Jake was still sick and to make things worse, three more hands told Zeke they were quitting.

"I'm awful sorry, Zeke, but I gotta look out fer me and mine," said Earl, who was the unofficial spokesman for the three of them.

"I know, Earl, Hell I know," Zeke said in a low, dejected voice, "And I ain't holdin' it again y'all either for wanting to light out of here. I reckon if it was me I'd do the same. I tell ya what, 5 years of killing and bein' shot at kinda changes a man's perspective on ownin' another man. I hope y'all can forgive me. Y'all know it ain't gonna be easy out there fer y'all but I wish ya God's speed!"

"I know that Mr. Zeke, we knows you're a good man, but we gots to find our own way out in this world now," Earl replied.

So that just leaves Marcus. He's now the only one left of the slaves/hired hands that Zeke had. No one knows what Marcus' last name is; his family had been bought and sold so many times over the years that they just kind of lost touch with who they were and where they came from.

Zeke was the last person to buy Marcus. He bought him about ten years ago. For years Zeke's family always owned at least a couple of slaves, and Zeke was no different. After he was married and starting out on his own farm, he went out and bought Marcus to help him. Something began to change over the years. Zeke began to see Marcus less and less as property and more and more as man. Just before the war started, Zeke agreed to give Marcus his freedom and asked if he would stay on as a hired hand. Marcus knew he had no education or future and if he left, someone else would surely snatch him up. Taking all that into consideration, along with the fact that Zeke and Elizabeth had always been reasonably good to him, he agreed to stay on and work for the McDaniels.

"I guess you'll be headin' out, too, Marcus," said Zeke.

"Nah, sir," replied Marcus. "You folks been awful good to me. I ain't got no other place to go. I can't read and I don't write none too good," he said.

"Marcus, I can't pay much at all," Zeke said.

"That's alright, Mr. Zeke. I don't need much," Marcus said with a big shiny smile.

"Alright, Marcus," Zeke said as he chuckled. Zeke was really happy to have Marcus stay on, but that didn't change the fact that there were only two men and one healthy boy to take care of this farm.

Christmas came and went without much celebration. January rolled around and nothing had improved. Jake really started to wither. He was losing weight. He could only keep down a little water and maybe a little bland oatmeal. Occasionally he would show a few signs of getting better, but then he would relapses and get sick again. Each time seemed to be a little worse than before. He was becoming more and more disoriented. Many friends and family stopped by from time to time to offer some old family remedy, but nothing seemed to help. Finally on January 13, 1866, Jake succumbed to complications from pneumonia.

His family was there by his side. Thomas was sitting in the corner with tears rolling down his face. Zeke became absolutely stoic. No expression at all. It was a combination of sadness, fear, and disbelief. Elizabeth, like any mother, was absolutely inconsolable . . . With tears streaming down her face, she grabbed Jake by his shirt and began to shake him.

"Wake up, wake up, Jake, please don't do this to me. Don't you leave me. No, Jake, don't you do this to me."

Zeke grabbed Elizabeth and tried to hold her close to him and console her. Marcus came running in from his room behind the barn. He had heard all the screaming. When he came in he quickly realized what had happened. Marcus was a big burly man but he had a very gentle face and it was easy to see how much he also cared for Jake. The two of them had become very close over the years, especially while his father was away during the war.

Zeke saw him come in and told him to take Thomas and go out to the barn.

"Yes, Sir," Marcus replied.

He helped Thomas up to his feet and put an arm around him as they went outside. Elizabeth turned and buried her face in Zeke's chest and wrapped her arms around him. On the outside, Zeke was trying to be strong but he too was dying on the inside. He knew the only reason Jake was sick was because he had him out in that bad weather trying to catch the stock that had gotten loose.

Marcus, knowing that someone would have to contact the undertaker, decided to handle it himself. He and Thomas saddled up and rode to town. When they got there they went to the home of the undertaker, Mr. Phillips. Mr. Phillips heard the pounding on the door and got up, lit a candle and made his way to the door.

"What do you want?" he asked.

Marcus took his hat off and said, "Mr. Phillips, Sir, we gonna be needin' ya out at the McDaniel Farm. Mr. Zeke's son Jake passed on this evenin'."

"What?" Mr. Phillips said in disbelief. He had known the McDaniels for many years. He knew that Jake had been sick but no one expected him to die. "Alright," Mr. Phillips said in a disbelieving voice, "Let me get dressed and I'll be out there as soon as I can."

After contacting the undertaker Marcus thought he had better let the sheriff know as well. They rode up to the office and went inside.

The sheriff looked at Marcus and said, "You lost, boy?"

"No, sir," Marcus replied, "I works for Mr. Zeke McDaniel. His youngest, Mr. Jake passed on this evenin'. I done stopped by Mr. Phillips' place to let him know. I just thought you should know too."

Sheriff Taylor went from a condescending to very compassionate look on his face. "Alright, you ride on back out there. I'll be out there directly with old man Phillips," he said.

Marcus and Thomas made the long painful ride back to the farm. Upon arriving Thomas put the horses in the barn and hung the saddles and blankets. Marcus tapped on the door as he walked in. Zeke was holding Elizabeth who was tightly clutching Jake's limp body.

"Mr. Zeke, sir, I fetched Mr. Phillips the undertaker and the sheriff, too," said Marcus in a low soft tone.

As he said that, the reality of what was happening sank in on Elizabeth and she began to cry harder again. Zeke stood up and looked at Marcus and nodded his head. He didn't want to accept reality either but he knew that was what had to be done.

"Thank you, Marcus, I appreciate you doing that for me. I really didn't want to leave Liz here by herself at home right now, especially with her and Jake in the same room."

"I know that Mr. Zeke, you need to be here right now with your wife and boy. Whatever you need, you let me know. I'll be alongside ya, Mr. Zeke," Marcus replied.

About a half hour later, Mr. Phillips and Sherriff Taylor arrived at the McDaniel's farm. They both solemnly entered the house with their hats in hand. Zeke greeted them in a low, defeated voice. Elizabeth was still next to the bed holding Jake and not acknowledging Mr. Phillips or the sheriff.

"I'm so sorry for your loss," Mr. Phillips said.   "That Jake was a fine boy; I know you both were awful proud of the young man he was growing in to."

The sheriff seconded what Mr. Phillips was saying. "Zeke, Elizabeth, I just wanted to offer my condolences too. We're here for y'all. We will try and help out with anything we can during these times. God almighty, this is something nobody ought to have to be going through," the sheriff added.

They were both trying to be as polite and thoughtful as possible, but when a parent outlives a child, especially a small boy, there are no words to sooth the soul.

Zeke went over to Elizabeth and tried to separate her from Jake. The harder he tried to pull, the more she resisted and cried.

"We have to do this, Liz. Liz, he is gone. The good Lord has called him home," explained Zeke.

She continued to hold on as tight as she could but when he said that, Elizabeth released Jake. She knew he was right. Zeke and Elizabeth both came from strong Presbyterian families, and they knew that it was the right thing to do. Although she was dying inside, she knew that our bodies belong to the Lord and they are His, not ours, to take when He is ready.

Mr. Phillips took little Jake's body outside to his wagon. Sheriff Taylor and Marcus helped load the boy and secure him.

The sheriff turned back to Marcus and said, "You do what them folks need you to do. They're gonna be in for a lot of hurt and pain the next few months. They're gonna need someone to help pick up all the slack around here."

"Yes, sir, I done told Mr. Zeke, I'm here for anything he and Mrs. Elizabeth needs," Marcus told them.

As the wagon started down the rough path back to town, Elizabeth fell to her knees in the doorway.   Zeke sat at the table with his head in his hands feeling completely lost and helpless.   The feeling of death had not left the house yet and both parents were consumed by it.   The feeling was so strong it was almost like a cloud hanging directly over them.

Thomas had stayed in the barn after he put the horses up.   He was standing next to a stall looking out the front door of the barn.   He had tears streaming down both cheeks.   Thomas was even more lost than his parents. He was having to deal with the loss of his brother and at the same time reconcile seeing his parents like this.   His parents had always been rock foundations much like all the other Scots-Irish settlers that lived in this area. He had never seen them so vulnerable and was having a hard time putting all this into context.

Zeke and Elizabeth were so distraught that they never even noticed that Thomas had stayed in the barn.   Marcus made his way back out there after tending a few things in the house.

"Mr. Tom, you best be getting back in the house, son," Marcus told him.

"No, I can't Marcus; I can't go back in that house right now.   I can't stand to see mama and daddy like this.   Plus I don't want to look over at Jake's bed.   I just can't look at it tonight, Marcus.   Can't I stay out here with you?" Thomas said.

Marcus reached down and put his hand on Thomas' shoulder.

"I reckon it'll be alright tonight.   I hope you ain't expecting to be too comfortable out here.   This ain't no antebellum mansion out here!"

Thomas broke a small grin and walked back into the barn with Marcus. They went back into the room that had been converted into Marcus's room. It was cool and dark but at least it was dry.   Marcus stoked the fire in the small wood burning stove and lit a kerosene lantern and hung it from a wire hanging down from a rafter beam.   Thomas had been in Marcus's quarters many times before but tonight was like seeing it for the first time.   He was seeing everything in a completely new light.   For the first time, he finally noticed how little Marcus had and maybe more importantly how well he did with so little.   He never complained; he was just happy to have a place to eat and sleep and stash a few belongings.   Thomas knew his family wasn't rich, far from it, but they were living pretty well before the war.

The next day started out as a cold, blue, blustery winter day.   The McDaniels woke up, although they never really slept that night, and began to dress.   Marcus hitched up a wagon and brought it to the front of the house. Hardly anyone said a word the entire morning.   A house that had always been filled with warmth and laughter was now eerily silent.   The cold from the winter weather was no match for the cold of death that permeated the home. They bundled up, loaded into the wagon and made their way into Anniston. They first stopped at the church and visited with Reverend Roberts, the local pastor. They wept and prayed and found comfort in his words.

Afterwards, Brother Roberts escorted them to Mr. Phillips funeral parlor. He had done a fine job preparing little Jake. He looked so calm and peaceful. Mr. Phillips had actually done such a good job that it made it even harder for the family to accept the truth.

"My God, Ezequiel, look at him, he just looks like he is sleeping. I just want to wake him up and carry him home," said Elizabeth.

"I know, Darlin'. I know it does but he's gone. We have to accept that."

Elizabeth looked up at Zeke after he said that with a look that was a combination of understanding but also "don't tell me what I can and cannot do!". Upon seeing the look on her face Zeke knew there was really nothing he could say or do that would make things any better, no matter how well-intentioned they were.

Word spreads quickly in a small town. Sheriff Taylor helped to inform the town of what had happened. One of the local families, the Jacksons, had quickly prepared a lunch for the McDaniels. Half of the town showed up to the Jackson house to pay their respects to the McDaniels as they tried to eat the meal that had been prepared for them.

"This meal is so good, Mrs. Jackson, but really y'all didn't have to go through this trouble," said Elizabeth.

"Mercy, child, it is no trouble at all, besides I couldn't face my maker knowing that I had not done my Christian duty!" Mrs. Jackson answered. "Really Mrs. McDaniel it weren't just me the whole town has been chipping in to make sure y'all have everything you need during this terrible time."

Zeke then adds, "Well it's awful good and we just want to thank all you ladies that helped, it has surely been a comfort to us, thank you!"

"You don't have to say a word, Mr. McDaniel, I couldn't imagine the pain you folks are going through right now. I just want to tell you our home is open if you need anything at all. If this damn war of Northern aggression wasn't bad enough now you have to deal with this loss, too. I just pray for you and your family," Mrs. Jackson told them.

Later that afternoon after the meal was served everyone gathered at the local church and Brother Roberts gave a very heartfelt sermon on the loss of a child.

"Friends, neighbors, what can we say about this fine young boy.   All of us knew little Jacob McDaniel.   He was as fine a creation as the good Lord ever sculpted.   But you see, friends, that's just it.   The little Jake you see layin' here before you is nothing but clay.   His soul is what's important, and I tell ya brothers and sisters, it ain't here no more.   It left this sick broken body last night and today is singin' and rejoicing with the Lord."

Brother Roberts went on to describe that Jake's earthly suffering is over.   His body remains but his soul lives forever in heaven.   After the service was over, the people slowly and somberly filed out of the church.   Everyone made their way over to the graveyard where the hole had already been prepared.   After a couple of verses of "Shall We Gather at the River" and "The Old Rugged Cross" Little Jake's body was finally laid to rest at the tender age of ten years old.

That night the McDaniels returned home.   They were functioning, but it was more like the undead than humans.   They hardly spoke a word to each other.   A few days passed and not much had changed.   Marcus handled as much of the workload as possible.   He was putting in 17 to 18 hour days, part of it was out of necessity, part of it was to relieve the workload off of Zeke and part of it was to keep his mind off little Jake who was like a son to him, too.   Elizabeth hardly left her bed.   Zeke and Thomas usually would just sit on the porch and stare off into the distance.

Finally, after about a week Zeke woke up and realized this couldn't continue.   As heartbroken as he was, something would have to give.   They could not continue on this way.   He still had to earn a living, and they all still had a life to live.   And as much as he truly appreciated the sentiment, he had gotten to the point where he could not stand any more well-wishers stopping by and having pity on them.   He got up and got dressed and asked his wife to do the same.   After they were all up and dressed, he told Thomas to go out to the barn and help Marcus with his chores.   Zeke and Elizabeth went for a walk.   It was a bright and sunny day which was typical for North Alabama in late winter but still a cool and very brisk day.   They started to walk out behind the house toward the little creek where they boys would fish and Elizabeth would draw water for cooking and cleaning.

"Now what, what are we gonna do, Zeke?" she asked.   Elizabeth was genuinely lost and confused.   There was no malice, hatred or sarcasm in her voice, she was just truly lost.   She had no idea what the next move for the family would be.

Zeke thought for a minute and then told her what he had mentioned a while back.   "Why don't we sack it up and git on outta here Liz?" said Zeke.

Elizabeth remembered what Zeke had talked about earlier, about leaving Alabama and starting over in a new place. At first it seemed like such an outlandish idea, but things had changed considerably since that last talk.

"I don't know Zeke? You sure 'bout that… just pickin' up and leavin?" she asked him in a timid voice.

"Don't rightly know, Liz, ain't sure 'bout too much no more," he replied in a monotone voice, "I do know this much, everything's changed. We lost Jake, lost our hired hands, looks like we gonna lose this farm. We gonna have to make some hard damn decisions woman."

"I don't know Zeke, God help me I just don't know," Elizabeth answered.

While Zeke and Elizabeth were talking at the creek, Thomas was talking to Marcus back up at the barn.

"What's gonna happen to us, Marcus?" Thomas asked in a very confused voice.

"Don't know, Mr. Tom, I sho' wish I did. I wish I had somethin' better to tell ya," replied Marcus in a lost voice. "I do know this much, Tom. Yo' ma and pa loves ya. They's gonna take care of ya. Yo' pa's a good man. One of the finest I ever did know. No matter what, he'll look after you and your ma."

Thomas began to feel a little better. Marcus had always been good to him. He was always there for a laugh or a little lesson in life. Thomas put a lot of stock in everything Marcus told him.

Meanwhile back at the creek, Elizabeth asked Zeke what he had in mind if they did leave the farm.

"If… and that's a mighty big If, we left Alabama, what did you have in mind?" Elizabeth asked her husband in a curious voice.

Now Zeke had been thinking about this off and on for the last few months. "You 'member when I wrote you them letters and told you 'bout a friend of mine named Sam Keller?" he asked.

"Sam Keller? Yeah, I believe I do recall the name now," Elizabeth answered.

"Well, old Sam's from Texas. When we wasn't too busy he'd get ta jabber whappin'' on and on 'bout Texas. Come to think of it, ever damn Texan I met during the war would just go on and on and on about that place. Anyway, he told me there's cattle down there runnin' wild and free as far as a man could see."

"Cattle runnin' far as a man could see, huh? That sounds like a load of hogwash, Ezequiel McDaniel!" exclaimed Elizabeth.

"Well, now I know it does, darlin'. I told him the same thing many times, but he says its cause all the men folk were away fightin' this damn God-awful war. They wasn't no one left back there but women and children. They can't take care of no ranch all by they lonesome. He said all them cows got loose from Mexico and ran wild all over Texas. He says they's gonna be a lot of money to be made there in Texas after this war was over," Zeke explained to her.

"I don't know Zeke; it sounds like a fool's errand to me," Elizabeth said in a very unsure voice. "I thought if we left here we could go to Tennessee or someplace like that. You know I still got some family there in around Knoxville and some around Greenville, South Carolina, some of Uncle Josh's kin are still there," said Elizabeth. "If we was gonna go somewhere, why not go back East where everything is settled and the Indians was licked?" she asked.

"Woman, ain't you been listnen' to what I told you a while back. Tennessee, South Carolina, Georgia, Virginia, it's all the same. Us and them Yankees blew ever farm and forest back to hell, from the Atlantic Ocean to East Texas and from Pennsylvania to Florida. They just ain't nothin' left here in the South. The problem is ever farmer and shopkeeper in the South is in the same situation. Ain't no one got a pot to piss in or a winder to throw it out of," snapped Zeke.

"Watch yer tongue, Zeke. There ain't no need gettin' all riled up. I was just askin'," Elizabeth snapped back.

"I know that, darlin', and I'm awful sorry. It's just that things have gone from bad to worse just about overnight and I'm pretty much at my wits'end," said Zeke.

"I know Zeke, me too," Elizabeth answered in a calm reassuring voice.

As they sat under a maple tree, Elizabeth thought more and more about what Zeke said. Her heart wasn't really into leaving. Alabama had been her family's home for the last forty years. She also knew that something had to give. Things just weren't looking up here in Anniston. She also couldn't bear the thought of going back into that house day after day and looking at the bed her youngest son died in.

"Tell me some more about Texas," Elizabeth told Zeke.

"Well, uh, like I said, theys cows as far as a man can see. And I hear tell it's about the most beautiful place you ever did see. I heard the stories of Sam Houston and Davey Crockett going on and on about how they ain't never seen nothin' quite like it, and theys both from Tennessee.   As far as the war goes, there wasn't a whole lot of it fought in Texas.   I believe they was a couple of skirmishes in far East Texas, but nothin' too much.   Not like we had down here.   Besides ol' Sam says most of them cows is in South and West Texas.   Ya know if ya think about it, darlin', folks have got to eat and people love beef.   Now that this war's over people's gonna start lookin' fer new land, movin' out West and rebuildin' the South.   Might not be a bad idea to get out to Texas first and stake a little claim for ourselves," Zeke told her.

What Zeke was saying made a lot of sense to Elizabeth.   She just was not convinced about Texas.   All she had ever heard about it was that it was a hard land full of hard people, Wild Indians, Mexican bandits, sweltering summers along with bitter cold winters in the Panhandle.   While they were sitting under the maple tree talking and thinking, Thomas and Marcus rode up.

"Everything alright?" Thomas asked.

"Yeah, son, everything's fine.   Don't you worry about nothin'," Elizabeth replied with a half forced smile on her face.

Zeke told Marcus to get down off his horse and join them under the tree. The four of them sat there the rest of the afternoon.   After a slow start, they slowly started to tell stories about Jake.   Then the stories turned into funny situations that he had always gotten himself into.   As the sun began to set the four of them were laughing hysterically, as well as therapeutically.

"Well I guess we best be gettin' back," Zeke told everyone.

"Yes, sir, Mr. Zeke, I reckon it's 'bout that time," Marcus answered.

Since Zeke and Elizabeth had walked down to the creek they doubled up with Marcus and Thomas for the ride back to the house.   When they returned home reality began to set in on them again.   The smiles and laughter from the afternoon were replaced with distraught faces and a dull ache in their hearts.

That night Elizabeth got everyone fed.   Usually, Marcus would cook for himself out in the barn, but Elizabeth insisted that he stay and dine with them in the house.   She prepared a fine stew with a big pan of cornbread and a big pot of coffee.   Everyone ate until they were stuffed.   After dinner, Marcus thanked her for the delicious meal and then asked to be excused.   He made his way out to the barn and built him a fire in his small wood burning stove to keep out the night chill.   Back in the house Elizabeth did the dishes and put everything away.   Thomas got ready for bed.   After bringing in an armload of wood for the night and breakfast in the morning, Zeke started to undress and get ready for bed himself.

That night everyone seemed to finally get a good night's sleep, everyone except Elizabeth. Even though she was still heartbroken about her son, her thoughts tonight seemed to focus more on Texas.

She thought to herself, "Is it the right thing to do? Can we make a life there? Can anything be worse than what is happening here?" Before she finally dozed off to sleep herself she looked up to heaven and prayed to God, "Lord, please give me the strength to deal with everything you put on our plate. I don't know why you took my baby from me, but I do know that you know best. I need ya, Lord. I'm lost and don't know what to do. Please be with us Lord, don't forsake us now, not when we need you the way we do. I pray these things in Jesus' name, Amen."

After saying that prayer Elizabeth seemed to find some peace and comfort. She too drifted off to sleep with the rest of her family.

The next morning Elizabeth was the first to wake up. She got up and built a fire. Soon Thomas and Zeke were awakened by the smell of coffee and bacon. The boys got up and stumbled their way to the table.

"Thomas, go fetch yer mama a pail of milk and tell Marcus to come in here and join us for breakfast," Elizabeth said.

"Yessum," Thomas replied in a half asleep voice.

After Thomas got dressed and made his way out to the barn, Elizabeth looked at Zeke and said, "Alright, Zeke, if you still want to go to Texas . . . I'm with ya."

Zeke looked up at Elizabeth from over his coffee cup and smiled. "You sure this is what you want?" he asked her.

"No...I ain't sure 'bout nothin' no more. But I do have faith in the good Lord and I do have faith in you. You made a whole lotta sense down yonder at the creek yesterday. I know there ain't nothin' left here 'bouts, and I don't think I can stay in this house anymore after losin' my baby. I'm with ya, Zeke. I am your wife and I will follow where you go."

Those words were music to his ears. Zeke never really thought he would convince his wife to leave Anniston much less Alabama. For the first time in months, Zeke felt like things might actually turn for the better.

Marcus and Thomas made their way back to the house and came in. "Awful kind of you folks to let me eat in here with y'all," Marcus said with his hat in his hand.

"Don't think nothin' of it, Marcus, you're a free man nowadays and you chose to stay. You've been a good hand and a good friend and we want you to know we appreciate what you been doin' for us these past few weeks," Elizabeth told him.

"Yes, ma'am," was about all the response Marcus could muster up with a halfway choked voice.   Marcus had been owned several different times and he had been treated badly by everyone else.   The McDaniels, even when they legally owned him, were never cruel to him and that was something that he never forgot.

As everyone sat down to eat breakfast Elizabeth asked Zeke to make his announcement to the family.   Everyone kind of stopped what they were doing and looked at Zeke.

"Alright," Zeke said as he set his cup down, "Well, Tom, Marcus, me and Liz been talkin' lately and, well, tryin' to figure out what we gonna do next, and uh, well what we decided is that we're gonna pack it up and move to Texas."

"TEXAS!" Thomas exclaimed.

"Yeah, boy, Texas," Zeke answered.

Zeke couldn't tell by the way Thomas said Texas if he was excited or upset.   The thing was that Thomas didn't know either.   It was a little of both. This was the only home he had ever known.   Then again there was nothing but misery here lately.   Thomas had also heard the stories of Davy Crockett, Jim Bowie, and Sam Houston.   He had heard about the wild Indians and the evil dictator Santa Anna.   All in all these stories made Texas sound like a mythical place that was out of reach for regular people.   He felt like it was reserved for those who were pre-ordained to live extraordinary lives.

Elizabeth broke in and said, "Me and yer pa have been talkin' 'bout this for quite a while now.   You're old enough to see what's goin' on here.   The markets have dried up, there ain't no money left here in Alabama or anywhere around here.   Your brother has passed on and some folks in these parts are starvin' to death."

She was right.   Thomas was old enough to see and understand what was happening all over the South.

Zeke then looked at Marcus and told him again, "Marcus, lots of men died to give you your freedom . . ."

Marcus cut him off right there and said, "No, sir, you gave me my freedom, before all this fightin' ever commenced.   I ain't likely to forget what you done for me, Mr. Zeke."

Zeke shook his head and said, "Okay, Marcus, but just the same, you are a free man now to go and do as you please."

Marcus looked off into the distance for a minute and then said, "I guess with this new freedom that all us Negros have . . . we can go and do as we please?"

"Yeah, that's the way I understand it, Marcus," Zeke answered.

"Then I choose to go to Texas, that is if y'all will have me with you."

They all smiled and Zeke said, "That's fine, that's just fine with us, Marcus."

The McDaniels decided to devote the rest of the winter to getting ready to make the move in the spring.   Luckily winters in Alabama are not that long. The rest of January and February was spent getting their affairs in order. They sold off things they wouldn't need.   Sold off all their stock and put the money under the mattress.   By the time the first part of March rolled around, they had saved all the money they could.   They were able to find a buyer for the farm.   Although they didn't get market value for that either, it was plenty to get them started on their way to Texas.

While they were loading up the wagon and getting the final preparations ready, Zeke began to think about something he said at the table a couple of months ago when he was telling Thomas and Marcus that they were going to move to Texas.

"Marcus, you 'member a couple months back when we first said we was goin' to Texas?"

"Yes, sir," Marcus replied.

"Well, I said something that I wanted to make sure you understand.   I said a lot of men died for you to have your freedom, and well, you know damn good-n-well which side I fought on but, uhh, well what I'm tryin' to say is . . ."

Marcus cut him off there, "I know Mr. Zeke, I knows what kinda man you is. I know you wore the gray because you felt like Alabama was yer country and it was bein' attacked by a bunch of folks that didn't understand what life's like down here in these parts.   I ain't never held it agin' ya, Mr. Zeke.   I know how you is.   I know what you really all 'bout.   I ain't got too much book learning, but I do know most them boys wearin' the blue wasn't interested in me being free.   They was just followin' orders, too."

"Yeah, I guess that's 'bout it, Marcus.   I just wanted to make sure you knew why I did what I did," Zeke said in a most sincere voice.

Elizabeth and Thomas made their way out to the wagon with the last bit of household items.

Zeke took one last look around the place and said, "Well that 'bout does it, I guess. We best get a move on, better not to look back once we get goin'."

Marcus and Thomas sat quietly. Elizabeth had a small tear in her eye but she was convinced the family was doing the right thing. As the mules pulled the wagon westward, the McDaniel Farm and young Jake's grave marker slowly began to fade into the distance.

After they had been in the wagon for a few hours it dawned on Elizabeth.

"Zeke, I know we're going to Texas, but where exactly are we going? I hear tell it is a mighty big state."

"We are headed for Prine, Texas, that's where Sam and his paw lived. He told me if I ever get out that way to look him up."

"Well, did you ever send him a letter telling him we were coming?" Elizabeth asked.

"Nah, come to think of it I didn't. But you know I ain't real sure how good he reads and writes anyway," Zeke answered.

Elizabeth began to giggle, "Oh Zeke, you just think of everything don't you!"

The Long Trail

Travel in those days weren't easy at all. First of all, there were no real roads to speak of and what was there was shot up or washed out. After a few days of ploddin' along they were in Mississippi. When they get to Vicksburg they decide to hold up and restock.

"Howdy, how y'all doin' this fine mornin'?" asked a local shopkeeper.

"Not bad at all," replied Zeke. As Zeke looked around he could see the ravages of war hadn't spared Ole Miss. "Looks like you fellers saw your fair share of that damn war too," Zeke said.

"Yessir, we shore as hell did. Whilst we's up there raisin' hell in Pennsylvania and Virginia, them other Yanks was down here blowin' my home all to hell," the shopkeeper exclaimed.

"I tell you what, them damn Yanks was thick as flies on molasses. Hell, you'd shoot one and two more would pop up. Damndest thing I ever saw!"

Zeke began to laugh, "Yeah, that sounds 'bout right. I fought up there at Gettysburg and I ain't never seen so much blue in all my born puttogethers."

The family all dismounted and went into the shopkeeper's store to stock up on what they needed. After the shopping was done, Zeke and the shopkeeper kept up the conversation about all the misery the war had caused.

"You know, Mr. McDaniel, I got shot in the ass,   my farm was burned down and my favorite mule went blind and fell off a cliff while I was gone, but that ain't the worst of. No sir! The worst part of this whole damn thing is that right there," the shopkeeper pointed out the window of his shop to a fancy dressed man walking down the street.

Zeke looked out the window and took a guess at what he was pretty sure it was.

"Carpetbaggers?" Zeke asked.

"Damn straight, carpetbaggers, I swear them sons a bitches is the devil on earth, I'd go as far calling them the 11th plague," the shopkeeper said with a fury in his voice.

The carpetbaggers had descended on the South at the end of the war. They were there for one reason, to get rich. They knew that most of the Southerners were in no position to demand anything and these people gobbled up land and homes all over the South. The Confederacy knew they lost the war and most of the people accepted it. But with these men coming down from up North and practically stealing their land it was like rubbing salt in an open wound.

"So where you folks headed, if you don't mind my askin'?" The shopkeeper said.

"Texas," Zeke answered as he took a swallow of his beer.

"Texas, what you all headed out that way for, got kin?"

"Nah, we lost everything back in Alabama. I had a friend back in the war, a fella from Texas. He was goin' on 'bout the opportunity out in that part of the country. We figured it would be a good place to start over," Zeke said.

"More power to ya....me....I'm gonna stay right 'chere. Mississippi has been my family's home for over three generations. I'll be damned if anybody's gonna run me off. Besides, everything I hear 'bout Texas sounds like a damn wild man's country. I'm a shade old to go out there and fight Injuns; I believe I've killed the last man I will ever kill, except for maybe one of them damn carpetbaggers!" the shopkeeper said as they both chuckled.

Zeke finished his beer and paid the shopkeeper. He stood up and thanked him for the supplies and hospitality. Elizabeth rounded up Tom and Marcus had the wagon loaded and ready.

"Where you folks stayin' for the night?" the shopkeeper asked.

"Ain't rightly sure, I figured we'd ride outta town a bit and look for a little place to camp," Zeke answered.

"Ah, hell, y'all set up your camp out here in this shed behind the store. It's supposed to rain this evenin' anyway," the shopkeeper told them.

"Well alright, we shore do 'preciate it," Zeke answered.

"Thank you so much, sir," Elizabeth added. "I sure don't fancy bein' soaked tonight," she said with her beautiful smile.

Marcus pulled the wagon around to the shed in the back of the store and unloaded a few things they would need for the night. The shopkeeper was right, just after sundown a heck of a storm blew in off the Gulf. High wind

"I don't know, son, I hope it holds a better tomorrow.   Hell, it can't be any worse than things has been this past year or so," Zeke said.

Tom kinda let out a halfhearted laugh at what his father said.   Tom knew his father was right, though. Things might be hard in Texas but things were absolutely horrible back in Alabama.   They hadn't been sitting on the river bank but maybe half an hour when Tom got his first bite.

"Watch yer line there, boy, I think yer gettin' a bite," Zeke told him.

"Yeah, I think yer right, Paw," Tom answered.

About that time that green hickory limb doubled over and the fight was on. Tom jerked the limb to set the hook and when he did that catfish tugged back trying to show him who was the boss.

"Hang on son, you got 'em now!" hollered Zeke.

The area where they were standing was on a slope with some loose sod. The more that fish pulled, the more Tom started to slide towards the river. That catfish gave one good jerk as he turned and tried to head out to deeper water.   When he did he almost took Tom with him.   Luckily for him, his father grabbed his suspenders just as he was about to take a tumble into the river.

"I gotcha boy, you just hang on to that pole," Zeke said laughingly.

Zeke held on to Tom and Tom held on to the pole and the fish held on to the hook.   After about fifteen minutes they were all exhausted but the fish was the first one to give out.   Tom pulled the line in steadily and when they finally got a good look at what was causing all that commotion they realized he had hooked into twenty-three pounds of thick, meaty flathead yellow catfish.

"Damn, son, that's a hell of a catch there.   You did just fine, son, that will be more than enough to feed all of us tonight;   maybe even some more for lunch tomorrow," said Zeke.

As they pulled the big fish in out of the water, they all three fell back onto the bank.   Zeke hit first, Tom landed on him and the fish landed on both of them.   They erupted in laughter.   The more they laughed, the harder it was to stop.   They lay there the better part of three or four minutes just busting a gut while that fish was slapping both of them frantically.

The laughter was a release more than anything.   There were months and months of hurt, anger, and depression built up in the entire family.   No one had really dealt with it, even the times they sat down as a family to talk.   That is a funny thing about life, though, sometimes the simplest thing, such as catching a huge catfish with your dad, can be all the healing and release you need.

The boys got up and dusted themselves off.   Zeke took both of the poles and Tom proudly carried his catch back to the camp to show his mother and Marcus.   "Well, how'd y'all do?" Elizabeth asked while still looking down at her Dutch oven. "Looky here, ma, look what I got," Tom hollered back to his mom.

Elizabeth looked up over the campfire and saw her son carrying a fish that was almost half the size he was.   "Lord Almighty, will you look at that. Tommy did you catch that one?" she asked.

"Yes ma'am," Tom replied.

"Ooohweee, that's a mighty fine catch there, Mr. Tom," Marcus said with that familiar smile of his.   "Come on boy let's go on down by the river and clean that monster."

Marcus reached into the wagon and pulled out a skinning knife and he and Tom headed back towards the river to clean supper.

"Did he really catch that fish himself?" Elizabeth asked her husband as he was putting the poles away in the wagon.

"He sure did, the only thing I helped with was keepin' him from fallin' in, but yeah he set the hook and landed him all by hisself," Zeke said.

A little while later Marcus and Tommy made their way back up to camp with several huge fillets of raw catfish in hand.   Marcus handed them off to Elizabeth and she proceeded to salt/pepper them and roll them around in corn meal.

That night as they had a hearty meal of catfish and cornbread they laughed and laughed as Tommy and his dad retold the story of how the fish almost drug him into the river.

"Y'all wanna hear a big fish story, well, I gots a big fish story for ya," Marcus said.   "My grand pappy and one of my uncles was fishin' up on the Tennessee River one day. They worked on a plantation that backed up to the river, and the owner used to let the colored folk fish down there when they needed some extra food.   Well, one day my ol grand pappy was in that river grapplin' for some fish."

"What's grapplin'?" Tom asked.

"Grapplin', well, that's when a man gets in the water and reaches up under them rocks and goes feelin' 'round fo' some fish."

"No way, Marcus, I know yer just joshin' me now," Tom said laughing.

"No, sir, it's the God's honest truth.   Anyway, my grand pappy was reachin' up under this big ol' table rock that done slid off in the water years and driving rain made life miserable for anyone who was caught out in it. The McDaniels, on the other hand, were high and dry and doin' fine.

The next morning the storm had passed but it was still a cool, cloudy morning. Marcus and Zeke loaded everything up and they headed out west towards the Mississippi River.

"How big is that Mississippi River?" Marcus asked.

"Don't rightly know Marc, I ain't never seen it. But I tell you what . . . if it's big enough for them river boats to go up and down it, it must be a powerful sight," Zeke answered.

They wouldn't have to wait long to see the Mighty Mississippi which was considered the unofficial start of the "West". People in Colorado and Arizona may argue that Louisiana and Arkansas aren't really in the West, but the river was a good geographical indicator none the less.

A major problem with not having good roads or road maps was getting lost, or at the very least, disoriented. When the McDaniels arrived at the Mississippi River, they ran into a pretty big problem. There was no way to cross it and the route they took didn't provide a ferry. It was too late in the day to start looking up or down river for a ferry so, they decided to camp that night on the river.

As they started to unload what they would need for the night, Zeke looked at his son Tom and then looked out on the river. "Say boy, it's been quite a while since we had us some catfish ain't it?"

"Yes sir," Tom answered.

"Tell you what, son, why don't you cut us a couple of hickory switches and I'll see if I can't rig us up some fishin' poles," Zeke said with a sly grin on his face.

As Tom went into the wood line to cut a couple of fishing poles, his dad dug through the wagon and found a roll of twine. He also looked through a box of miscellaneous whatnots. He found two old fishing hooks. When Tom returned he gave his dad the poles. While Zeke was putting the fishing poles together, Tom went out and found a nice moist piece of ground and dug up some worms for bait.

While Tom and Zeke headed down to the river bank, Marcus and Elizabeth continued to unload what they would need for the night and set up a makeshift camp.

"What do you think, Marcus, what would go good with some fried catfish?" Elizabeth asked.

"I tell you what, Miss Liz, some of that good cornbread you make would sho' 'nuff hit the spot," Marcus answered with a wide bright smile.

"Alright, cornbread it is!"

Back down on the river, Tom and Zeke sat quietly staring at the lines in the water, waiting for the first sign of catfish lurking in the area. Zeke looked at his son and noticed a faraway stare on his face.

"What's ailing' ya boy?" Zeke said with concern.

"I don't know, Paw; I guess it is just everything. Seems like it all happened so fast don't it?" Tom replied.

"Yeah, it shore does," Zeke answered.

"Paw....do you think God don't like us? You know, he let Jake die, we lost the war, we lost the farm, all yer hands quit. Just kind of seems like God don't want us around sometimes don't it?" Tom asked his father.

"Nah boy, you got it all wrong…God don't hate nobody. Hell, even Lucifer himself was God's favorite angel at one time. We just run on a string of bad luck that's all. I know it seems like the end of the world sometimes, but you got to remember there's folks out there lot worse off than us. We got a chance to rebuild a life in a new place. One of them exciting places like you read about in them dime novels. Texas is gonna be something like you ain't never seen. And as for Jake, well, I miss him something powerful but I do know this . . . one day we'll see him again and we'll never get split up again. If we quit loving the Lord and following what the good book says then we would never get the chance to see him again and I sure don't want to do that," Zeke tried to explain to his son.

"Yeah, Paw, I guess you're right, I ain't really thought on it like that, but I guess we really ain't got much choice," he replied.

"Nah, son, that's the hand we been dealt and we just gonna have to play it out and see what happens next."

Zeke looked down at his son and put his arm around him and told him how much he loved him. Tom looked up and managed a smile himself. They both knew it wouldn't be easy, but Tom realized his father was not about to give up so he figured he couldn't quit either.

After a couple of minutes Tom looked up at his father and said, "What do you think Texas is gonna hold for us pa?"

ago.   My uncle Rufus was watchin' from the bank, all the sudden my pap' hollers, 'I gots me one, Rufus, I gots me one.'   'Bout that time my ol pap disappeared into that ol' dark murky water."

"What happened?" Tom asked.

"Well, Mr. Tom, one dem big ol' bluecats latched aholt a his arm and jerked him straight down to the bottom.   He pulled up once and took a big ol' gasp of air and down they went again.   My uncle Rufus jumped in to help him out but ol' pap was well on his way down the river locked onto that ol' blue.   Finally, Uncle Rufus got out of the water and ran 'longside the bank tryin' to keep up. They stopped up at a deep hole bout fifty yards from where they started. Rufus jumped in with his ol' green river knife and went to stabbin', after a couple minutes he kilt that ol' blue and my pap could finally come up for air. They drug that fish onto the bank, took both men to get it out.   When they got it back to the cabin they weighed it on a cotton scale.   That ol' boy weighed in at ninety-five pounds."

"I'm sorry, Marcus I just can't swallow a story like that," Tom said.

"I knows just how you feel there, Tom.   I felt the same way when I heard it but my ol' pap rolled up the sleeve on his right arm and showed me a row of scarred skin made from bluecat teeth!"

"Are you serious?" Tom asked.

"Boy if I'm lying may the good Lord just come on down and get me now!" Marcus replied, putting one hand in the air and the other on his heart.

"Well, I reckon that's bout enough stories for one night," Zeke said as he got up to put his plate away, "We gotta get an early start in the mornin' so we best get some shut-eye."

"Night mama, 'night pa, night Marcus," Tom told everyone.

"Night boy," his father answered.

Everyone slowly began to settle in for the night.   Zeke and Elizabeth made a bed in the back of the wagon and Tom and Marcus under the wagon.

The next morning was a bright and shining one.   After a breakfast of bacon and biscuits they loaded up the wagon and found the nearest ferry and took it across the river.   Once they were on the other side, the journey to Texas continued.   The next week or so went on without any real incidents to speak of.   After a few days of crossing through Louisiana, they finally reached that Texas border.

"Howdy," Zeke hollered out from his wagon to an old man patching a hole in his pirogue. "Is this here Texas?" he asked.

The old Cajun looked up at him and said, "No, sir, but you ain't missed it by much, the Texas border's down that way 'bout twenty mile or so."

"Looks like somethin' got a hold of yer flat bottom there, mister," Zeke said curiously.

"That's fo' sho', mister. 'Bout a week ago I was polin' this here pirogue down the bayou yonder ways. I been out checking my trotlines, when all 'da sudden without no warnin' atoll the biggest damn 'gator I ever did see locked down on the front of this here pirogue and commenced to tear that front end all to hell, I tell you what!" the old Cajun exclaimed.

The whole McDaniel clan kind of looked at each other then they looked back at the old Cajun.

"You mean to tell us that a 'gator did all that damage to your boat?" Zeke asked.

"Oui, monsieur, I do, and this here's a pirogue, it ain't no boat, a boat's what you mountain folk be ridin' in. Down here in dees parts it called a pirogue," said the old Cajun.

"And you lived to tell it," Zeke said with a half grin on his face.

"Bec mon cul," said the old Cajun. Zeke looked at the old man with a confused look on his face. "Dat mean 'kiss my ass!' " the old Cajun replied, "My name is Edward Louis Delacroix and they ain't no 'gator round dees parts that want no part atoll of Big Ed Delacroix."

With that everyone busted out into a huge laugh. Everyone needed to blow off a little steam and Big Ed Delacroix was just the man to help them do it.

"Well, y'all hungry?" Ed asked.

"Yeah, I 'magine we could eat a bite," Zeke replied.

"Me too. I got me an ahnvee for a mess of jambalaya!" Ed said. Once again everyone looked at Ed with a lost look on their faces. "Dat mean I'm hungry, too. What's da matter y'all don't speak English?" with that Ed started laughing uproariously.

The McDaniels sort of looked at each other again and began to giggle themselves, wondering what kind of company they'd run onto this time.

That night Big Ed asked them why they were heading for Texas.

"Well, between the war and bad luck, we have pretty much lost everything that ever meant anything to us.   We figured we'd head out west and try our luck out there.   I know an old boy out in Texas that I served with during the war," Zeke explained.

"Poo-yee-yi (that stinks)!   That damn war caused more trouble than it was worth," Big Ed answered.

"Did you serve in the war, Mr. Delacroix?" Elizabeth asked.

"No, ma'am, I was right 'chere where I belonged.   I had no part in what them boys was tryin' to do.   Damn shame, though, them Yankees couldn't just leave folks be."   As he said that he looked at Marcus and thought about what he had just said.   "I don't mean no disrespect.   I been huntin' and fishin' dees swamps for nigh on thirty years or so.   Lots of niggers back here, most of 'em pretty good folk.   Whatever my pa didn't teach me 'bout swamp runnin' them niggers did, so's I got no problem with 'em.   I just think the government should leave folks be."

Trying to lighten up the mood a little bit, Tommy asked big Ed about the alligator incident, hoping he would tell them the whole story.   "Mr. Delacroix, what exactly happened again with your boat, I mean, pirogue?"

"Well, boy, bag daer (back there) 'bout two mile up that bayou I had me a trotline set out.   I know they's a yellow cat 'least fifty pounds in there.   I been baitin' that hole for two months tryin' to snag that sumbitch.   Well, I nosed my pirogue up near the bank to re-bait that hook.   I had my back turned and didn't see that damn monstrosity 'til it was too late.   All I heard was the damnedest crunch you ever did hear.   'Bout that time the pirogue commenced to shakin'.   I turned around and seed that gator and I let out with a yell, 'Laissez les bon temps rouler, you son of a bitch.' That means let the good times roll, and I tell you what the fight was on!   He kept chompin' on the nose of my pirogue and I commenced to whoopin' his 'gator ass with the business end of my pole.   By the time it was all done there was blood, sweat, tears and 'gator shit all over the bank of that bayou. I was plum tuckered out and he was dead.   We lay down on the bank next to each other.   My shirt was torn asunder and his brains was bashed out.   But I tell you what . . . that night I had me the best 'gator stew in the wide world, I gauronteee!   I did learn me one good lesson that day….don't ever, ever leave a lot of blood drippin' off the side of your pirogue.   I been cuttin' bait all day and they was blood and guts all over the bow.   Some of it must have been drippin' off into da water.   Woo, Lord, I don't make that mistake two times!"

By now the McDaniels were rolling on their sides.   Not just because of the story, but because of the flair the old man had for telling a story.   Whether everything he said was true or not, well, doesn't really matter.   The bottom line is it was a good story and it sure made the night fly by.

The next morning, about daybreak, Elizabeth woke up first and started to build a fire for coffee and breakfast. As the fire was up and roaring and the smell of bacon and coffee wafted through the cool morning air, Big Ed came wandering through the woods and back to camp.

"You scared me," Elizabeth exclaimed, "I didn't know anyone else was up and around."

"Yes, ma'am, I don't believe in sleepin' in too late, makes a man lazy. Besides, I had some traps to check this morning," said Ed.

"Well, sit down and have some coffee. Breakfast will be ready directly. Do you take milk and sugar Mr. Delacroix?"   Asked Elizabeth.

"Zeerah (disgusting)," said Big Ed in a playful voice.   "Milk and sugar, that's ok for mountain folk, but down here in the swampland we take it straight!"   As he took his first sip of coffee he leaned back against a log and said, "Joie de vivre, yes ma'am that is the joy of life, a good cup of coffee in the mornin'."

About that time Marcus and Zeke began to move about.   As Zeke pulled on his suspenders, he told Marcus to give Tommy a kick and get him out of bed.   Marcus playfully reached out and kicked Tom in the butt.

"Wake up there, Mr. Tom, we burnin' daylight."

Tommy let out with a groan and a sigh.   "Is it morning already?"

"Sho' 'nuff, smell that breakfast your mama's cookin'.   Come on.   Let's get a move on.   We got a long day 'head of us.   Texas is just down yonder road," Marcus told him.

Once breakfast had been finished and the wagon was loaded, Zeke stuck out his hand and told Big Ed thanks for the hospitality and the supper.

As he did that Big Ed handed him a bag and said, "Here's a lil' lagniappe for you!"

"What's that?" Zeke asked.

"It just means a little somethin' extra for y'all, for your trip," Ed told them.

Zeke opened up the bag and looked; Ed had given them a bag full of boudain sausage for the trip.   "Thank you kindly," Zeke said with respect and appreciation.

"Bonne Chance (good luck)," Big Ed told them.   He knew they would need it traveling through Texas.

After a short journey, they finally hit East Texas. "Well, I ain't exactly sure where we hit it, but this is Texas. I know we've been over twenty miles now," Zeke said.

"Looks pretty much like Louisiana," Liz replied.

The truth is there isn't a whole lot of difference between Western Louisiana and Eastern Texas. It's all pretty much pine forest, swamps, and high humidity.

Other than the Caddo Indians and a few misplaced Cajuns there wasn't a whole lot in East Texas. The McDaniels figured that out pretty quickly. The next several days were spent trying to find a path to fit their wagon through in the midst of the dense forest.

They finally caught on to the El Camino Real trail that led them out of the East Texas wilderness and into the present day Austin area.

They stopped and set up camp on the Colorado River and Elizabeth told Zeke they were running low on some supplies. "Zeke, we're gettin' a little shy on flour and coffee."

"Alright, I'll send Marcus on in to Austin to fetch us some...Hey Marcus...," Zeke said. "I heard ya', Mr. Zeke, I'll get my stuff unloaded and I'll be movin' out," said Marcus.

Marcus finished unloading his gear and then he started out down the river heading to Austin. Later that night Zeke, Liz and Thomas were eating their supper.

"Hey, Paw, shouldn't Marcus been back by now?" asked Thomas.

"Yeah, I figured he would. I didn't think Austin was that far down the river. But I wouldn't worry too much, I 'magine he'll be back by breakfast."

The Hill Country

Well, the next morning rolled around and Marcus hadn't returned by the time Liz was up making breakfast and boiling coffee. Zeke and Tom began to load up the wagon.

"What do you think happened, Paw? Marcus still ain't back."

"I don't know, son. I figured he'd come ridin' in by now," Zeke answered, "Well, we'll be ridin' into town pretty soon. We'll either run into him on the trail or we'll find him in town."

After breakfast was finished and the last of the dishes were packed, the McDaniels were on the trail for Austin. About two hours later they reached the first settled parts of Austin.

"Well, family, I reckon this here's Austin," Zeke said.

"I hope so," said Liz, "It seems like it's been a coon's age since we were in a civilized place."

Thomas then said, "Paw, I don't see Marcus anywhere, do you?"

"No, son, I don't. Soon as we get settled in somewhere we'll commence to huntin' him," Zeke told Tom.

They found a small area behind the livery stable to pitch their camp. While Elizabeth was unloading the wagon, Zeke and Tom went through town looking for Marcus.

"Where do you want to start, Paw?" Tom asked.

"I 'magine the best place would be at the general store. That's where I would have gone first," Zeke answered.

Zeke and Tom went inside the local general store. There they were met by a jolly older man. "Howdy, you folks just into town?" asked the store keeper.

"Yes, sir, just now rode in this morning," Zeke told him.

"Well, it's nice to meet you folks.   Name's Henry Jones.   Been here in Texas since old Steve Austin was selling land plots down here.   What can I git y'all today?"

"Well, we do need a few things, but one of my hands rode into town last night and was supposed to pick them up and we ain't seen him since.   I was wonderin' if you'd seen him by chance," Zeke told Henry.

"Well, what did this feller look like?"   Henry asked

"He was a big negro fella.   About 50 years old and wore an old slouch hat with a pair of faded overalls," Zeke told him.

"Yeah, seems to me there was a big old nigger in here yesterday buying some stuff.   He caused one hell of a commotion though," Henry said.

"How's that?   Marcus is a quiet man, he ain't no trouble maker," Zeke said.

"Well, me personally, I got no problems with niggers.   They're folks just like anyone else, and their money is green as any white man's or Mexican's. But we got a few people 'round these parts that don't see it that way at all," Henry told them.

"What happened to him?" asked Zeke.

"Well, these two old boys followed him in the store and they confronted him.   I told them I didn't want no trouble in my store, and they told me to shut the hell up and shoved me aside.   That nigger of yours said he didn't want no trouble either and that he'd be ridin' out of town just as soon as he could get these supplies.

"Well, that wasn't good enough for these old boys.   They jumped him and I guess that was their first mistake because that old boy of yours commenced to whoopin' the hell out of both of them old boys.   I tell ya it was actually pretty funny.   The only problem is folks in the street . . .   all they saw was this big nigger whoopin' two white boys.   Someone got the sheriff and he came running over with his deputies and put a stop to the whole thing.   They arrested your boy and I ain't seen him since."

"Where did they take him?" Zeke asked.

"Over yonder to the jail I 'magine," Henry answered.

"Tom, you stay here and git the supplies for yer ma'.   Once you git 'em ride back over to the camp.   I'll be along directly."

"Where you going, Paw?" Tom asked.

"I'm goin' over to have a talk with the sheriff.   Now you git them supplies like I told ya."

Tom got the supplies that his mother needed and went back to the camp as he was told.   Zeke, in the meantime, made his way over to the sheriff's office to have a talk with him and find out what had happened to Marcus.

"Howdy," said the sheriff as Zeke walked through the door, "What can I do for you, sir?"

"Two fellas jumped a man in the general store yesterday.   I want to know where he is and what happened to him," Zeke told him.

"I don't recall no fight……..oh…….you mean that nigger who jumped Pete and Otto Schmidt," said the sheriff.

"That ain't how I heard it and I want to know right now what y'all did with him," Zeke said with a stone face.

"Stranger, I don't believe I got your name," the sheriff said.

"McDaniel, Ezequiel McDaniel."

"Well, Mr. McDaniel, my name is John McNally; I am the sheriff of Travis County.   What's your business with that nigger?   I know he ain't a runaway slave.   Them damn Yankees made sure of that," Sheriff McNally said.

"No, he ain't no runaway.   He works for me.   He gives me a fair day's work and I pay him a fair wage.   He also happens to be a good friend.   Now I'm getting real damn tired of explaining myself and not getting any answers," Zeke told the sheriff.

"Now you look here, Mister, no one rides into my town, comes in my office and starts telling me what's what," the sheriff said.   Sheriff McNally was doing his best to sound tough but those that really knew him knew he was long on talk and short on action.   He liked to bluff his way through life.   After he threatened Zeke, Zeke continued to look into his eyes with a steel resolve. Sheriff McNally "flinched" first and he sort of smiled.

"Well, it's like I said, Mr. McDaniel.   He jumped Pete and Otto.   So we ran him in.   I released him this morning.   On his way out of town I did notice Pete and Otto trail along after him."

"What did you do about it?" Zeke asked him, in half disbelief.

"Nothin'.   There ain't no law against two fellas ridin' out of town the same direction someone else rode out on.   Besides, I reckon them boys just wanted to make up for any kind of misunderstanding there might have been yesterday!"   The sheriff said with a sly grin.

Zeke knew it was pointless to argue with this poor excuse for a sheriff, so he rode out in the direction the sheriff had pointed at.   In no time at all Zeke saw Marcus's horse along the wood line. He rode over quickly and started to call for Marcus. He heard no answer as he checked over Marcus's horse to see if it was okay. All of a sudden he heard a slight moan. Zeke didn't see anything but he called out again to Marcus. He heard another strained moan coming from some tall grass near a clump of oak trees.

"Oh Lord, Marcus, are you alright?" Zeke could tell that Marcus was not alright. He had been worked over really bad. Pete and Otto had gone around Marcus and then ambushed him as he rode past. Once they got the jump on him they could handle him a little better than they did back at the general store. The boys took turns and took their time beating on Marcus. As if the beating wasn't savage enough, they pinned a note into the flesh of his chest when they were done. The note read, "Niggers not welcome."

Zeke pulled the pins out of his skin and threw the note to the side. "Come on Marcus, we gotta git you some help."

Zeke loaded up Marcus across his horse and then led them both back into town.

When Zeke got back to town he found the local doctor's office and he grabbed Marcus and kicked the front door open.

"AHH!!" screamed the sleeping doctor, as Zeke kicked open the door. "What the hell happened to him?" the doc asked.

"He was ambushed," Zeke replied.

"Well, here, get him on this table so I can have a look at him."

Zeke did as the doctor said. After he got him on the table Zeke stepped back and let the doctor have a look at him.

"Lord, looks like this fella pissed off the wrong old boy," the doctor said.

"Being black ain't against the law," Zeke said.

"No, sir, I guess it isn't," the doctor replied. The doctor was sincere. It was just a stereotype that everyone in the South and even out West was racist. The doctor saw everyone as equal, and he worked just as hard to save the life of a black man as he would to save the life of his own mother.

The doctor continued to work on Marcus for the next hour or two. By now Elizabeth and Tom had made their way over to the doctor's office to see how Marcus was doing.

Liz asked, "Will he be alright, Zeke?"

"I don't know yet. That doc seems to be a pretty good old boy and he's doin' his damndest to fix him up," Zeke replied.

About that time the doctor stepped out of the office onto the wood plank sidewalk where the McDaniels were still waiting.

"I never did get yer name, mister," the doc said.

"Ezequiel McDaniel, but most folks just call me Zeke. This is my wife Elizabeth and my boy Thomas."

"Well, it's nice to meet you folks. My name is Dr. Ed Tomkins."

"Dr. Tomkins, will Marcus be okay?" Liz asked.

"I don't know yet, ma'am. It is still too soon to tell. I think he will heal up from those bumps and bruises, but the cut where that pin was put in his chest is infected. I have him on some medicine but we will have to wait and see how his body reacts. You know, Mrs. McDaniel, a lot more men died from infection than from Yankee bullets in the late War Between the States," Dr. Tomkins said. Zeke knew what the good Dr. said was right, but that was not subject he cared to relive so he changed the subject.

"Dr. Tomkins, what can you tell me about these Schmidt boys. They's the ones that jumped Marcus," Zeke said.

"Well, they're 'bout as worthless as tits on a boar hog. Oh, please excuse my language, ma'am," the Dr. said.

"That's okay, Dr. Tomkins, I am not a pampered woman," she replied.

Zeke told Elizabeth and Tom to go back to the camp. He was going to the saloon to have a drink with Dr. Tomkins and discuss the Schmidt boys. Elizabeth agreed but Tom wanted to stay with his dad. Not that he was scared; he was mad, just as mad as his father was.

"You go on back to the camp, boy. You help yer ma out. I'll be along directly; I just need to find out about these fellers. Don't worry son. We'll get them boys that did this to Marcus. I swear that one on the good book," Zeke said.

Tom and Elizabeth rode back to the camp and waited for Zeke to return. Before they left Liz asked Dr. Tomkins, "Would it be okay to come in and check on Marcus occasionally?"

"Why sure, ma'am, you come on in as often as you like. The door will be open, I also got some fresh bandages on the desk if he needs them," the doctor. Told her.

"Well, how about that drink, Mr. McDaniel?" Dr. Tomkins asked.

Zeke and Dr. Tomkins made their way over to the saloon.

"Give us a bottle, Jim," Dr. Tomkins hollered out to the bartender. The bartender brought over a bottle of Tennessee sour mash and two semi clean glasses.

"I'll pour, you talk," Zeke told the doctor.

"Well, I know the Schmidt boys, like I was telling you over at the office. They are pretty worthless. They're German immigrants, just like most of the folks in these counties round here. Most the immigrants are honest, hard-working Christians. But these two, I don't know what happened.

"Their ma died in Germany, I believe. That's the reason their pa came to Texas. But he was killed by bandits when them boys was 13 or 14 years old. After that they didn't really have anyone to watch over them and keep them on the straight and narrow. They grew up as wild as a peach orchard bull. I reckon a lot of that meanness just comes from missing their folks."

"Well, dead parents or not, that ain't no excuse for what they did to Marcus," Zeke said.

"No sir I don't reckon it is," the doctor replied, "What do you plan to do about it?"

"I'm gonna find 'em and kill 'em I 'magine."

"Well, sir, some people, like the sheriff, may look at that as murder," Dr. Tomkins said.

"Well, Doc, I met your sheriff this morning and I wasn't too impressed, to say the least. I'll tell you this, though. I'm usually a peace lovin' man, but if he tries to stop me then I got no problem takin' him out, too," Zeke replied.

Zeke and Dr. Tomkins finished their drinks and Zeke headed out to the Doc's office to check on Marcus. Marcus was conscious but not very coherent, to say the least. Zeke told him not to worry that there would be justice. The people that did this would pay for it; he swore his honor on it.

After visiting with Marcus, Zeke headed back to their makeshift camp behind the old livery stable.

"Well, what did ya find out, Ezequiel?" Liz asked her husband.

"Well, found out a few things. Doc Tomkins is a pretty good old boy, I wouldn't piss on that sheriff if he was on fire, and I found out who those Schmidt boys are. They don't know it yet but the wrath of God is about to descend on 'em come morning light."

"Now, Ezequiel, I don't want no trouble, we're just passin' through these parts," Liz said.

"Woman, did you see what they did to that man? I wouldn't treat a dog that way. And don't forget, he may still die, we don't know yet," Zeke said.

"I know, I know…..I know what yer sayin', Zeke, but this ain't the way to go about it. Besides the good Lord says 'vengeance is mine'," she told her husband.

"Yeah, well, that may be true, wife, but the good book don't say nothing 'bout who He'll use or how He'll deliver that vengeance," Zeke told her in a dead serious voice.

This argument went on for a while. Elizabeth never did agree it was a good idea. After five years of war and a dead son, she had dealt with all of the death and destruction she cared to for a lifetime; but with that being said, she also knew there was no way she would ever convince Zeke to change his mind. The war had not made Zeke bloodthirsty, but he was always a man who stood ramrod straight and fought for what he believed was right. The only thing the war had done to him was deaden some of the human feeling that comes along with killing.

The next morning Zeke got up before sunrise, saddled his horse and rode out of town. The doctor had told him where their farm was just outside of Austin. About the time the sun was up in the sky real good, he rode up on their little spread.

"Hello the house………Hello the house," Zeke hollered towards the front door.

Pete Schmidt opened the door, not knowing who Zeke was, "Can I help you Mister?" he asked.

"Is this here the Schmidt farm?" Zeke asked.

"Yes it is, what's it to you stranger?" Pete asked.

"Well boy, I'll cut the bullshit and git straight to the point. I came here to kill ya."

"Kill me? You must have me confused with someone else Mister," Pete yelled back from the house.

"You 'member that old boy in the general store that y'all jumped the other day, that was my field hand. His name is Marcus, and he ain't dead yet, but it don't matter none, 'cause here in about two minutes you and your worthless brother will be," Zeke hollered back.

"Well hold on minute there, Mister," Pete said as he leaned back slowly from the door to reach for a rifle leaning on the wall.

As Pete tried to make his move, Zeke drew first and dropped him with one shot from that old .44.   Pete flew backwards into the cabin, crashed into the table and lay there with his eyes lifeless and blood streaming from the corner of his mouth.

Just as he shot Pete, he heard another shot coming from behind him.   He whirled around with his pistol cocked.   All he saw was Otto Schmidt leaning against the barn wall and spitting up blood.   As Otto fell to the ground, Zeke saw Sheriff McNally standing behind him with smoke still coming from the barrel of his old Sharps rifle.

"What the hell are you doing here?" Zeke asked.

"Well, I heard what you was planning on, and I just couldn't let you take the law into your own hands like that,"   Sheriff McNally replied.

The truth is Sheriff McNally knew all along what Zeke was planning on doing.   After thinking long and hard on it, the Sheriff thought he could save face by acting like he was still the one in charge instead of allowing some stranger to come into town and start running things.   Besides the Schmidt boys gave him a good excuse.   No one around Austin liked them much anyway.   And there was plenty of things they could be run in for.   The Sheriff figured he could kill two birds with one stone.   He could look like he really was in charge of the town, as well as getting rid of two troublemakers.

"I'm obliged to you for doing that," Zeke told him.

"Forget about it, but you can do me this favor, if anyone asks you, I legally deputized you this morning before you rode out here,"   The Sheriff said.

"Fair enough," Zeke replied.

"Now, there is something you can do for me.   Get your family, get your nigger and get out of Austin.   Y'all are a headache I don't need round here," the Sheriff said.

"We'll be ridin' on, just as soon as Marcus can ride, but I ain't leavin' till then.   You're hired to protect folks in this town and you did a piss poor job with Marcus.   So we'll be staying till he's good, then we'll be putting our backs to you,"   Zeke told the Sheriff.

Now that Sheriff McNally knows Zeke means what he says he agreed they could stay in town until Marcus was well enough.

About a week passed, and Marcus was slowly starting to heal up.   The medicines had helped and the infection had died down.   The McDaniels loaded up and picked up Marcus and they headed west out of Austin.

The Nephew, Charley Dalton

While the McDaniels were making their way through Texas, some of their family had already beaten them there, actually by several years. Charley Dalton was the only son of Zeke's sister Katherine.

Katherine and her husband Henry were poor, small-scale farmers like most other people in mid-19th century Alabama. Henry and Charley left Alabama in the spring of 1855 after Katherine died. They headed out to Texas to try and, not so much forget about her, but to start over in a new place where there weren't so many reminders.

Henry and Katherine were a loving couple. Neither of them had much but they had each other and that always seemed to be enough. They had a 20-acre farm that always seemed to produce just enough cotton to sell and raise enough hogs and chickens to feed the family. They were proud and hardworking. Their only escape was church on Sunday and the occasional town social or fishing trip. Other than that, like everyone else, most of their time was spent in the fields or doing household work.

Katherine had been working on a plot of land that she was going to turn into a garden. It was early in the spring and she was just beginning to break up the land for planting. In what was a terrible, freak accident, there was a copperhead snake lying in the grass. Katherine didn't see it as she reached down into the grass. The snake struck lightening quick. She screamed and drew back her hand but the damage was already done. The viper had landed both fangs in the webbing of her right hand. She called for help as she tried to get back to the house, but Henry and Charley were both gone. They had left earlier in the day to look for a hog that had rooted out from its pen during the night.

Kate's hand began to swell and turn black. She tried to run to the house which raised her heart rate and continued to pump the poison through her blood stream. She made it out of the tall grass and back close to the house but it was too late. As she gasped for air, her eyes rolled back in her head and she stumbled and fell down face first in the dirt.

A couple of hours later Henry and Charley returned home with a rope on the hog's neck being led from the back of Henry's plow mule.

"Kate, we's back!" He hollered again, "Katie girl, you in there?" There was still no answer. "Charley, go look and see if yer ma is still working on that little garden spot," Henry told his son.

Charley hopped down from the mule and started running back to where the garden was supposed to be. All of a sudden he let out a blood-curdling scream.

"Paw, hurry, quick Paw, ma's hurt bad!"

Henry turned loose of his mule before he even put him away. He took off running as fast as he could to the back of the house. When he got there he saw Charley kneeling down with his ma's head in his hands.

"She won't wake up, Paw, I tried but she just won't open her eyes," Charley said through the sobs.

Henry looked down and saw the black swollen hand and two red marks on it. "Oh, no," he said low and under his breath. "Oh, God, no," he said a little louder.

"Son, go in the house and get me a blanket," Henry said as the tears were now rolling down his own cheeks. Charley ran into the house like he was told to do. Henry held his wife close to his chest and began to wail, but as soon as he started he also tried to rein it in because he knew he would have to be strong for his young son.

Charley came running back out of the house, hoping against hope that his ma may have opened her eyes while he was gone. When he returned his paw looked at him and told him, "She's gone, son, a snake must have bit her while she was clearing out that land over there. I don't even know if we could've done anything for her if we had been here."

"No, No, Paw, that can't be. She just can't be gone, it's not fair," Charley said sobbingly.

"You're right, boy, it ain't fair, it ain't fair at all, and I don't know why the good Lord would take her from us now," Henry replied.

"Why don't you do something? Daddy, do something!" Charley was screaming and yelling at his father whose face had gone stoic. Charley threw the blanket onto the ground and ran away from the back of the old house out towards the pasture.

"Charley, Charley come back, get back here, boy, do you hear me?!" Henry screamed. Charley ignored his father and kept running as fast as he could towards the woods at the far end of the pasture. Henry gently laid his wife's lifeless body to the ground and took off after his son.

"Charley, wait, stop boy, and stop!" He kept running until he finally caught up with the young boy half way across the pasture. He came up swiftly behind Charley and grabbed him, tightly clutching him in a bear hug from behind. Charley was inconsolable and Henry was clueless, not knowing what to say or do to reach his son. Finally, after a couple of minutes, Charley turned around in his father's arms and they began to cry and hug each other. Henry fell to the ground tightly hugging his young son. Finally after what seemed like an eternity, but likely only a few minutes, they got up and slowly walked back to the cabin.

Henry loaded his wife's body into a wagon and rode into town. They stopped by the local undertaker and then went to their local church. They made all the necessary arrangements then they headed back out to the farm. Some friends and family had stopped by to bring food and offer condolences. A few people stayed the night with them on the farm so they wouldn't be alone. Those who stayed the night were only trying to be helpful; they cooked a big meal for the boys and cleaned up the cabin as well as putting away some of Katherine's personal things.

The next morning Henry and Charley both dressed up in their best white shirts and cleanest overalls they could find. They both wore a tie under the overalls and cleaned up their brogan shoes the best they could. With slicked down hair and sad faces, they got into the wagon and headed back into town to do the hardest thing they would ever have to do in their lives.

After an obviously gut-wrenching funeral, they loaded up and headed back to the farm. A lot of the same friends and family rode back out to comfort them. Throughout the rest of the day everyone offered advice. Everything from remarry quickly, to bury yourself in work, to go to church more often. Henry thanked everyone for the help and hugged and kissed everybody as they left.

That night Henry and Charley were sitting at the table. Charley was drinking a cup of milk and Henry was pulling on a jug of sour mash.

"Git yer stuff boy, we're leavin'," Henry said.

"Where we headed, Paw?" Charley said with a confused look on his face.

"I don't know, west, just….west," he answered.

Under the cover of night, Henry and Charley loaded everything they considered essential into their wagon and headed west. They didn't have a whole lot to take: a young bull, a milk cow, four mules and a sorrel horse. They fashioned a couple of wooden cages to take a few Dominecker hens. The wagon had a couple of guns, a family bible, some extra clothes, blankets and a few keepsakes from his beloved wife.

As the sun came up to their backs the next morning they had already put 12 miles between them and their farm. Unlike the McDaniels, Henry had absolutely no idea where he was going or when he would be there. He had no plan and very little money. All he knew was he wanted out. He knew he would lose his mind and kill himself if he stayed in that same house. He also knew he had a young son who was depending on him. If he killed himself what would happen to Charley? He would probably end up in some orphanage and he wasn't about to let that happen.

About a month later in Mid-April, the Daltons crossed the Sabine River and were officially in Texas.

"Hey, Paw, how 'bout here? They say once you cross the Sabine you are out of Louisiana and in Texas. I've read some stories about folks who came to Texas because they wanted to start over again, plus they say Texas has a little bit of everything. They say if you want a new start, Texas is the place to be," Charley said.

Henry looked around the landscape as he held the reins loosely. "Nope, I ain't interested at all, son, this Eastern part of Texas looks just like Alabama. We'll keep ridin' west. If this whole damn state is nothing but pine forests, we'll just keep on ridin' west to the New Mexico territories or all the way out to California if we have to. I just don't want to be anywhere that looks or sounds like where we came from," Henry told Charley.

After a couple more weeks of traveling, Henry definitely noticed a change in the landscapes.   It went from the dense forests of Alabama, Louisiana, and East Texas to a more open rolling hilly country.   Henry thought real hard about stopping in West central Texas near what would be present day Coleman and Brown Counties.   But he hadn't quite outridden the hurting of losing his wife.

They made camp one night on the Colorado River in what would be Southern Coleman County today.

"What do you think about this country here, Charley?"

"Pretty nice country, Paw, lots of water, plenty of oak trees and lots of good black dirt,"   Charley answered his father.   As Henry lay there next to the campfire he tried to decide if this was far enough west.   He got some unexpected help from an Indian raid led by a Comanche chief named Santa Anna.

They seemed to strike from out of nowhere.   The first arrow hit the campfire and slung coals all over young Charley.   He screamed and yelled "Indians!"   Henry yelled for him to get in the back of the wagon.   Charley jumped in and reached for the rifles.   All they had was three .50 caliber muzzleloaders and two black powder pistols.   Luckily it was a small raiding party.   Charley threw his Paw a rifle.   Henry got off his first shot and dropped an Indian as he rode in.   For a young boy of 12 Charley was no slouch himself, he fired a shot and gut shot another Indian as he came storming in. Charley gave his dad the last rifle and he then began to reload the other two.

Henry dropped his sights on an Indian with the third rifle.   As he was about to pull the trigger an arrow sliced his left thigh open.   It was just a grazing blow but it was enough to drop him to his knees.   As the Indian rode up on him he jumped down and tried to take his hair but Henry was able to fight him off and beat him down with the butt of the rifle.   Charley took one of the pistols and shot another Indian who had rode in to help.   By that time Santa Anna had decided to retreat when he realized these farmers wouldn't scare too easily.

"Are you okay, Paw?" Charley asked.

"Yeah boy, I'll be alright.   It just cut the outside of my leg.   Here take this kerchief and tie it around that cut real tight."

Charley did as his pa told him.   They rested for the rest of the night and at first light they tried to put as much distance as they could between them and Santa Anna's stomping grounds.   A couple of days later they rode into Fort Concho in San Angelo and began to ask about the Indians in the area.

The commanding officer began to explain that West Texas was some of the wildest, woolliest untamed land in all of America. "Mr. Dalton, you have to understand the majority of white settlers live around Austin and San Antonio and a few German and Czech communities around that area. Once you start getting out west of the Texas Hill Country and the central part of the state, you are really in no man's land.

"There are some U.S. Calvary units stationed from South Texas in Brackettville near the Rio Grande to Ft. Richardson in Jacksboro up in North Texas. Governor Elisha Pease still has some Rangers riding around to help settlers out against Indians and Mexican Bandits, but you have to understand we are all few and far between. Mr. Dalton, you and your son would be better off to ride back east and maybe head down south to Austin."

"No," Henry answered. "I just came from back east, and I already grew up in the South. No, sir, we are headed west. Come hell or high water we are going to settle out farther west."

"Why, sir, may I ask, are you so smitten to keep moving west?" the army officer asked him.

"Well, sir, it really ain't none of your business. I don't mean no disrespect because I know you're just looking out for settlers, but still, there ain't no law that says I can't keep moving west is there?" Henry said, already knowing the answer.

"No sir, of course there is no law forbidding westward movement. I am truly only telling you this for your safety. Anywhere west of this line we simply cannot guarantee your safety and that of your young son," the officer told him.

"Let me ask you this; could you absolutely guarantee me and my son's safety if I turned around and went to Austin or San Antonio or New Braunfels?" Henry asked. "You mean to say if I only go back east of here and settle down I will not be attacked by Indians, or Mexican bandits or anybody else?" Henry added.

"No sir, I could not guarantee that nothing would happen east of here either," the army officer told him with a defeated look on his face.

Henry then smiled a bit and slapped the officer lightly on the shoulder, reinforcing that he understood the army was just looking out for the well-being of travelers but that he and his young son were determined to keep going no matter the cost. Maybe it was because San Angelo was not the right place for them or maybe Henry had a bit of a death wish and didn't care if he and his son were murdered but no matter the real reason they pushed on ahead.

Henry and Charley spent most of the rest of the money they had on supplies to get ready to leave out of Fort Concho.   "Why are we going to keep going, Paw?"   Charley asked.

"Son, if we go back East, we are just going to be going back to where we come from.   If we push on out west, we may be able to get past this Indian trouble and finder a little better place to live,"   Henry answered.

The next morning after a big breakfast Henry and Charley loaded up and left the Concho Country and headed deep into West Texas.   The next week or two found more Indian trouble and lots of gaps between water holes. Finally, they pushed into Presidio.   For those of you who don't know, Presidio, Texas, looks nothing, absolutely nothing, like Northern Alabama.

"What river is that Paw?"   Charley asked.

"It is the Rio Grande, chamaco," said a weather-beaten vaquero.

Henry turned his head to see who was talking to Charley.   "Howdy," Henry told the Mexican man.

"Buenos Dias," said the Mexican.

"Yeah……uhh….Howdy," said Henry again.   "Do you speak English?" asked Henry.   The Mexican replied, "Didn't you just hear me say, 'It is the Rio Grande'?"

"Oh yeah.………I guess you did," replied Henry.   Henry got down from the wagon and stuck his hand out, "My name is Henry Dalton, that there is my boy Charley, we come from Alabama."

"It is nice to meet you.   My name is Vicente Suarez, but people just call me Chente," the Mexican answered them.

"Did I hear you say that is the Rio Grande?   Well, I'll be a suck-egg mule, that means on the other side is Mexico, right?"   Henry asked.

"Si, Senor, that is Mexico over there.   Why do you ask?"

"Well, I've been ridin' west looking for a new place to settle down. I didn't figure that we'd pushed this far out.   Hell, I guess this is gonna be home from here on out.   It don't look nothing like Alabama, water is damn shore scarce in these parts, and I don't speak no Spanish so I reckon I better stay on this side of that creek.

"Chente, how's the farming out in this part of the world? Ya'll git much rain out here?" Henry asked.

"Senor, look around you . . . do you really think we get much rain? This is not farm land. You can grow a little for yourself but you will never make a living like you did back East. The elevation is too high, the rain is too little and the rocks are too many. God did not make this land for the plow. No, senor, he made it for las vacas y caballos," Vicente answered him.

Henry looked at Chente with a confused look on his face.

Chente smiled and said, "The cows and horses, God made this country for the cows and horses."

"'Scuse me fer askin' but how'd you learn to talk English so good?" Henry wondered.

"Well, senor, my father Don Fernando Suarez was the best vaquero in Northern Mexico; no one could match his skill on a horse. He was also a smart businessman and he knew the American soldiers needed horses.

"There are many, many wild mustanos, mustangs, they are excellent horses for this part of the country. My father wanted to round them up and sell them to the Americanos, but he did not speak a word of English. When I was a young boy he would take me to white settlements and forts to learn all that I could and slowly I learned the language enough to deal with the soldiers on the horse sales. Over the years I got a little better and a little better.

"I took my father's advice and when I had my own son I talked to him in English as much as I did in Spanish. Now my son Mario speaks perfect English as well as his native tongue.

"Senor you are more than welcome to settle in Presidio. It is a wild country with much untamed land. If you wish to become a vaquero instead of a jardinero I will be more than happy to help you start a new life here," Chente said with a big smile on his face.

Once again Henry looked at Chente with a big confused look on his face. Chente laughed again. "I said I will be happy to teach you how to be a cowboy instead of a farmer!"

Chente invited Henry and Charley to stay and work at his ranch while they were getting settled in. Chente introduced his son Mario who was Charley's age and his wife Antonia. The two boys hit it off and became the best of friends. As for Henry, he was a little slower to come around. Henry was born and raised in the Deep South. He was by no means a wealthy landowner but had owned a slave or two from time to time. You wouldn't describe him as a white supremacist by any means but he was ambivalent to most nonwhite people.   Chente Suarez was the first Mexican he had ever met in his life, and he wasn't quite sure what to make of him.   He seemed like a nice enough man but he kept asking himself, "what were Mexicans like?"

They say that time changes everything and that was no different for Henry and Chente.   Henry was grateful for the opportunity that Chente had offered him.   Henry never said a cross word to his boss.   He often wondered if it was out of respect for the man who was helping him and his son or if it was out of fear of getting on the wrong side of a man who represented the huge majority in this part of the world.   Either way, Henry got up and worked hard every day.

He had a few culture clashes with the other vaqueros on the ranch but it was nothing too serious, and it was usually chalked up to cultural ignorance and not hatred of any kind.   Slowly over time, Henry discovered a new and genuine respect for the people of this land.   He soon learned how hard working and honest they were, not to mention that they knew more about raising horses and surviving in the rugged mountains of West Texas than anyone else.

As time passed by, Chente and Antonia helped the Daltons get on their feet and carve out their own ranch not far from the Suarez ranch.   Henry and Charley raised cattle and goats but horses were their specialty.   Chente passed on everything that his father had taught him about rounding up and herding horses and many other time-tested vaquero traditions.   Henry was no greenhorn himself.   He had grown up around horses and knew quite a bit himself.   He had broken and shod many a horse, back in Alabama.

After a few years, the Daltons had their own ranch up and running with a pretty steady income coming in.   The only thing that was really missing was a wife.   Henry thought about it but most of the girls in West Texas were Catholic and Henry was a foot washin' Baptist.   Besides, he just never quite felt right about sharing his bed with another woman.   Let me rephrase that; he never felt comfortable sharing the bed long term.   There were a couple of overnighters every once in a while but checkout time was usually early the next morning.   And it wasn't like Charley was doing without a ma completely. Antonia had practically adopted him and treated him like one of her own. Anyone who has ever been around those nice Mexican ladies knows what I'm talking about!

Over the years Charley and Mario both grew up into fine young men. They both had a nice spread to their shoulders, and both were tougher than boot leather. They might raise a little hell every now and again but you couldn't ask for better sons who would always be there for you when the chips were down.

In the mid-1860s business was booming for all the horse traders in the area. The South needed horses and Henry, Chente and others were more than happy to oblige. Henry had a special interest in the war. Being a native of Alabama and reading what was happening back East, he took it really personally. To Chente on the other hand, it was purely business. He really didn't care which side won. He was a free Mexican, and he would kill, or die trying, anyone who came and tried to take that away. Besides most of those problems were way back East; from East Texas to Virginia and Tennessee down to Florida. He just felt like it was too far away to ever affect West Texas and the Big Bend area.

Charley was somewhere in the middle, he sympathized with his dad because he took it so personal, but then again he agreed with Chente that all that was way, way back East and wouldn't affect them out here. And being partially raised by Mexicans, he had no sympathy for what he considered racists, even though he knew not everyone in the South was that way. He knew that most of the people who fought for the Confederacy were fighting for states' rights and not for slavery. But sometimes it was hard to separate the two.

In 1865 that bloody war finally came to an end. When it did all the money was gone out of the South, and people were starving. Henry started going farther into Mexico to sell horses than he used to. It was out of necessity. At the time a peso was about as good as a dollar.

One day Henry told Charley, "Son I'm headed 'cross the river to sell a few head of these horses. I got a couple of cowboys from town to help me drive 'em down. We art to be gone a week or so. I need you to stay here and tend them two mares that are pregnant."

"Yes, sir," Charley answered.

Henry and two other cowboys took off across the river splashing towards Mexico and rode off towards the sunset. Charley finished his chores on the ranch and rode over to the Suarez ranch to see if he could rustle up a free meal. A week came and went, and Charley continued working on the ranch, tending the mares, and drinking a few beers in town.

As Charley stepped into the local cantina, a shout came from behind the bar, "Howdy, Charley. Has yer paw come home yet? I got me a couple of green broke ponies I need shod," said the bartender.

"Naw, I ain't seen 'em yet. I figured he'd been in last night but I guess he run on a little senorita down there in Mexico," Charley answered.

They all had a good laugh. Charley sat at a table in the corner and had a couple of beers and shot the bull with some local cowboys. Even though he had been joking about it, he really began to wonder what might be holding his paw up. Old Henry took his horse trading pretty seriously. And even though he liked a little whiskey as much as the next fella, he usually didn't let it get in the way of his business schedule.

A few more days came and went and Henry had not shown up yet. Charley decided to saddle up and go look for himself. He crossed the river and headed towards that little village where the horses were supposed to be sold. After a couple of days of riding, he rode up on a sight that no child should have to see, especially twice in the same lifetime. Henry and his horse were lying there bloody and dead.

Charley rode up on him. It was obvious Henry had been there a couple of days. Charley broke down just like he was a 12 year old boy again holding his mother's head. Once he stopped crying, he took a knife and a metal plate and began digging a shallow grave for his beloved father. After a few hours of digging, he wrapped his pa in a blanket and laid him in the ground. He built a cross out of mesquite limbs and said a heartfelt prayer. The only comfort he found was the knowledge that his beloved pa and his saintly ma were finally reunited in heaven.

Charley's sorrow soon turned to rage as he grabbed his horse and continued into the town where his pa was headed. That evening he rode into town totally consumed with revenge. He walked into a cantina and began asking questions. Over the years Charley had become quite fluent in Spanish himself.

He began to ask what happened to the gringo who had the horses. It wasn't long before he began to get some answers. It turned out the two cowboys Henry picked up in Presidio were actually planted there and were working for a horse rustler from Del Rio. Word had gotten round that Henry was making a good living as a horse trader and some unscrupulous people wanted to get in on what Henry had worked for.

Charley had wondered why three cowboys left Presidio but only one was lying there dead in the desert. While Charley was getting the answers he wanted, the swinging doors opened and in walked Mario Suarez.

"Mario, what the hell are you doing here?"

"I'm looking for mi hermano (my brother)," Mario answered.

"This is different, Mario, this ain't got nothing to do with you," Charley said.

"You've got a lot of nerve talking to me like that Carlitos (Charley). Somos familia y tu lo sabes bien (we are family and you know that)," Mario answered.

Charley stood up from the table and looked Mario in the eye. He never said a word; he just stumbled out the door past Mario. He got on his horse and rode out of town. Mario walked out of the cantina and got on his horse and followed him. Mario caught up to Charley lying under a big cottonwood tree a mile or two out of town.

Mario dismounted and looked at Charley, "Right, now my mother is at church, lighting a candle, crying and praying for your safety. My father is sitting in the barn drinking tequila wondering where his best friend is. They both fear the worst for your father. They hope that I can find you and bring both of you back safely.

"I am sorry for your father; he was a good man and a good friend to our family. There is a time when you can't distinguish friends from family. You and your father crossed that line with us many years ago. You are as much a Suarez as I am; you're just not as good looking."

When Mario said that, Charley couldn't help but laugh. "Carlitos, I want vengeance for your father just as much as you do. I loved him, too. You tell me what we need to do and you and I, together, will deliver God's justice!"

Vengeance

Charley accepted his friend's offer to help track down the people who murdered his father.   Henry was as good to Mario as Chente and Antonia were to Charley so Mario felt he had a stake in what happened to Henry.

"What have you found out so far?"   Mario asked.

"Not much," Charley replied while staring blankly into the campfire.   "I talked to some people in the cantina in town, and they told me two cowboys rode in with a string of horses.   They was ridin' in from Texas.   Then they left east out of town yesterday."

"Did they say where east?"   Mario asked.

"No, but I figure maybe Del Rio.   They gotta sell them horses somewhere, ain't a whole lot of towns 'tween here and there.   Besides Fort Mckavet's down that way.   They might try to sell 'em to the soldiers," Charley said.

"Well, hermano, do you have a plan?" Mario asked.

"Sort of, I plan on spending the night right 'chere then headin' south at first light.   I'm gonna ride to Del Rio, find them boys, and blow a hole in 'em big enough to drive a team of mules through!" Charley replied.

"I guess that's a plan," Mario said, pushing his hat back and scratching his head.   Mario went to his horse and pulled his saddle down and untied his bedroll.   As he rolled out his bedroll Charley poured him a steaming cup of coffee.   The boys lay down under the tree staring at the stars and sipping on the coffee.   They both had a lot on their minds but neither one said a word, to himself, or to each other.

The next morning as the sun first peeked over the eastern horizon, Charley and Mario were both saddling their horses.   As Charley pulled his cinch down tight, he looked at his best friend and asked if he was ready to ride.   Mario looked back at him as he tied down his bedroll and nodded yes.

Before the sun was completely over the horizon, the boys were making tracks east towards Del Rio.   Three days later the boys crossed the Rio Grande and rode into Del Rio.   The first night they rented a room in a small hotel and lay low.   They had a good meal of steak, beans, and tortillas with a large mug of beer to wash it down.   The boys drew no attention to themselves.   After they ate and had a couple of drinks they retired to their room.

The next morning they came out of their rooms and they started around town asking questions.   Mario went to the livery stable and began to ask about two strangers with a string of ponies.

"Howdy, how are ya, this morning?" said Bill the livery stable manager.

"Good, gracias, how are you?" Mario replied, "I'm looking for two cowboys with a dozen horses that may have come through here a few days ago."

"Yeah, seems there was a couple of old boys that rode in last week with some horses to sell.   It was some damn fine lookin' stock.   I been workin' horses since I was knee high to a grasshopper and I'll tell you them was about as good as any as I ever saw.   You're too late, though, a couple of big ranchers were passing through and bought them mustangs on the spot as soon as they seen 'em," Bill told Mario.

"I ain't lookin' to buy the horses, I'm lookin' for those vaqueros," Mario replied.

"Friends of yorn?" Bill asked.

"No, I plan to kill them if I find them," Mario said.   "They killed my best friend's father and stole his horses."

Bill looked at Mario with a surprised look on his face, but he could see that he was not joking.   "Well, best I remember them fellas live 'round these parts. I believe they work on a ranch just east of town.   A fella named Pete O'Reilly moved here from Ireland about 10 years ago.   No one round these parts trusts him.   He ain't never been charged with nothing but seems like he's always got his hands in some dirt.   One old boy's name was Tel Savage and the other fella was D.L. Campbell.   I never cared much for them fellas, but I never figured them for killers," Bill said.

Mario thanked Bill for the information.   He jumped on his horse and rode to the other side of town.   Charley was standing on the front porch of a dry goods store talking to a couple of other people.   When Charley saw Mario riding up, he asked if he had found anything.   Mario nodded his head and motioned for Charley to follow him.

Charley tipped his hat and thanked the old boys sitting on the porch.   He jumped down and mounted his horse.   Mario took off east of town and Charley followed along behind him.

"Well, what did you find out, hoss?"   Charley asked.

"I talked to the man that runs the livery stable; he said he knows those hombres.   He said the vaqueros' names were Tel Savage and D.L. Campbell.   He said they worked on a ranch for an Irishman named Pete O'Reilly who is a known horse trader in these parts;   they also said he's usually up to no good," Mario said.

"Well, where abouts is this ranch?"   Charley asked.

"East of town is all he said," Mario answered.

"Well, Mr. Suarez, let's light a shuck out that way and pay them boys a visit," Charley said.

"Cuidado hermano (careful brother)," Mario replied, "We don't know where these guys are at or what they look like or how many there might be of them."

Charley realized what Mario was telling him made a lot of sense, but he wasn't about to be put off by the facts as they started riding out of town towards the general direction of the O'Reilly ranch.   Soon they rode up on a rundown adobe house with a little old Mexican man working a plot of soil out front.

"Buenos dias, senores," the old man said.

"Buenos dias, como estas?" Mario replied.   "Buscamos el rancho de Pete O'Reilly?"   Mario said.

"Pete O'Reilly, si, si, es alla en el otro lado de la Montana," the old man said.

Charley looked over and said, "The other side of that mountain, huh?"

Mario tipped his hat and told him thank you and goodbye in Spanish.   He and Charley took off to the other side of the mountain that the man was pointing at.   Once they crossed to the other side, they stopped and took cover on the hillside and scouted out the ranch to see what they were up against.

"Que piensas (what do you think)?" Mario asked Charley.

"Well, I don't see anybody at the ranch house, but there is a couple of fellers out front of the bunkhouse," Charley said.

"Well, let's don't over think it, let's just ride down and ask their names.   If it is them, let's just kill them," Mario said.

"Yeah, that sounds good.   I was thinking the same thing," Charley said.

Charley and Mario hopped on their horses and rode slowly downhill.   They rode up to the ranch and went over to the bunkhouse.

"Howdy," Charley said.

"Howdy," the two cowboys replied.

"My name is Theo Wilson and this is my partner Rudy Gonzalez," Charley said, trying to think of a couple of names as quick as he could.

The cowboys nodded and replied, "My name is Tel Savage and this here's D.L. Campbell.   What can we do for you fellers?"

"Not much, just say howdy to the devil for me when you see him," Charley said.   As soon as he said that, Charley and Mario drew their pistols quick as lightening and shot both men.

Mario shot Campbell in the head killing him instantly.   Charley shot Savage in the gut because he wanted to try and get some answers.   He hopped down and grabbed Savage by the shirt.

"My name is Charley Dalton.   My paw was Henry Dalton . . .   you know old Henry, that horse trader y'all went to Mexico with here while back."

Savage lay there breathing heavily with tears running through his handlebar mustache.   "I'm sorry, boy, I swear I'm sorry, Mr. O'Reilly he done put us up to it.   He said he wanted some of that stock.   He wanted to sell them mares and keep them studs for his own stock.   He's the man you really want.   Please, son, don't kill me."

Charley let go of Savage's shirt and stood up.   Savage lay on the ground whimpering.   Charley cocked his pistol and pointed at it Savage's head and pulled the trigger one more time.

"We gotta go, hermano, if we stay here too long they're going to start coming down on us," Mario said.

Charley and Mario lit out and rode back to Del Rio to lay low for a while. The boys rode through Del Rio and crossed into Mexico to find a little place to camp.   They thought they would wait there to see what O'Reilly would do next.

The boys didn't have to wait long for a response.   That night O'Reilly and some of his other cowboys came riding into Del Rio.   They were looking for a Mexican and a white boy who were in their early twenties.   Most of the townspeople didn't want anything to do with O'Reilly and his boys.   Most of them were honest about it.   They simply said they hadn't seen anything or anyone.

Pete O'Reilly ended up riding all through town leaving his message.   He told all the townspeople if they saw these boys they needed to ride out to his ranch and let him know.

He also gave the town an idea of what he had in store for them when he caught them.

The next morning right at dawn, just as the sun was breaking, Charley rode into town and slipped into the back of the livery stable to talk to Bill who was still asleep in the hayloft.   Charley climbed up and poked old Bill in the side.

"Ahhh!" Bill screamed.   Charley quickly put his hand over Bill's mouth to shut him up.

"Boy, you scared me out of ten years of good growth, what the hell's wrong with you?" Bill whispered in a very loud voice.

"Hush, Mister, my name is Charley Dalton, you talked to my friend Mario yesterday 'bout them two cowboys that killed that man and stole his horses."

"Boy you must have a set of cojones the size of cantaloupes; do you have any idea how big a pile of shit you and that meskin boy are in?" Bill asked. "What the hell did y'all do yesterday?"

"We rode out to that Irishman's ranch and killed them fellers.   That O'Reilly feller wadn't there or I'd a killed him too," Charley told him.

"Son, I can appreciate ya tryin' to avenge yer pa, but, boy, you ain't gonna make it out of this one alive.   That Irishman would slap the shit out of a wildcat and not even bat an eye.   The last ten years he's been here, he's planted enemies the way farmers' plant oats," Bill told Charley.

"I ain't worried 'bout that.   I believe I got the upper hand on that old man," Charley said.

"How you figure that, son?" Bill replied.

"Cause he ain't ever rode up on anybody like me!" Charley said with a cold, steely look in his eyes.

Bill went on to pass on the message that Pete had left for the boys.   He had heard it all in the cantina last night while he was in there drinking.   He also said that O'Reilly should be at the ranch house today.   The last few days he had been way on the far back side of his ranch checking on some cattle with some of his hired hands.   Since he was in town last night, he should be around the next couple of days.

Charley tipped his hat and told old Bill he appreciated the information.   He climbed down out of the hayloft, grabbed his horse, and slid quietly out the back of the livery stable.   Charley rode quietly out of town.   Once he hit the edge of town he sunk spur and had his horse at a high lope.   He rode hard all the way back to the spot where he and Mario were camping.

When he got back Mario was already up and had a fire going with a pot of coffee boiling and some bacon cooking in a small pan.   There were also a few 'day old' biscuits warming on a rock.

"Well, what did you find out, hermano?" Mario asked.

"I guess I found out everything I need to know," Charley answered.

"I talked to old Bill at the livery stable, and he told me that Pete O'Reilly rode into town last night telling everybody what all he had planned fer me and you when he caught us."

After a quick bite to eat, Mario and Charley packed everything up, saddled up and crossed the river back into Texas.

"'Mano, have you thought this one out?"   Mario asked.

"No, not really," Charley answered.

"It ain't gonna be that easy, 'mano.   We caught them by surprise yesterday.   Today they will be barricaded in, locked, loaded and waitin' for us," Mario told him.

"Yeah, I know.....," Charley said in a low voice.

"I got an idea, when we get to the ranch you stand out there and holler at the house to get their attention.   I'll get up on a hill looking down on the house.   If he steps out onto the porch, I can get him with my rifle," Mario said.

"What the hell am I supposed to do?" Charley asked.

"Duck.......quickly," Mario said laughing.

When the boys rode up close to the ranch they split off.   Charley continued to ride on towards the front of the ranch, and Mario started up a hill that would look down on the house.   The closer Charley rode to the ranch, the more he began to think and second guess himself.   The more he thought about Mario's plan, the more scared he became because he was definitely putting his head on the chopping block.   At the same time though he thought about what had happened to his father.   He was gut shot and left to die alone in the Mexican desert while a couple of lowlifes rode off with his stock and trade.   The rage he felt for his father soon began to take over and bury the feelings of fear he had from his best friends 'well-laid plan'.

As Mario rode up the side of the hill he was doing some thinking of his own.   He was a good shot, but was he good enough to hit a man from several hundred yards?   He knew he didn't want to let his best friend down. He was also really close to Henry, so he wanted just as much vengeance. Not to mention, if he missed, his best friend would be standing there as a wide open target for O'Reilly and his men.

Mario got to his area first and settled into a good spot to look down on the house.   Charley rode up to the front entrance of the ranch.   He paused for a moment and took a deep breath.   He couldn't see Mario so he hoped to hell he was already in position.   Charley gave his horse a small kick and the horse started to lope a little closer.   After getting a few feet closer he hollered.

"Hello the house!" No one answered.   "Hello the house, you pile of Irish chicken shit!"

The front door of the house opened slowly.   Two cowboys stepped out onto the porch.   Charley and Mario were both upset because they wanted Pete to step out so they could get this over with.

"Whachu doin' here, boy?   Don't you know what we got planned fer you?" one of the cowboys asked.

"I ain't got no beef with you fellers.   I'm lookin' for O'Reilly," Charley told them.

The cowboys looked at each other and giggled a little bit, then they looked back at Charley, and they both went for their pistols.   Mario fired from the hill and dropped the nearest cowboy instantly.   Charley pulled his pistol and wounded the second.   As the second cowboy raised his gun to fire back at Charley, Mario fired his rifle again, killing him too.

As the shootings began, several other cowboys scattered from the ranch house, the bunkhouse, and the barn.   Soon there was a flurry of bullets headed towards Charley.   He decided that retreat wasn't so bad of an option. As he rode off he was able to kill one more and wound another.   Mario was able to kill two more from the hilltop before he jumped on his horse and rode out.

Charley and Mario met up at the place they had originally split off from.

"'Mano, come on, we got to get the hell out of here," Mario said.

"You ain't got to tell me twice!" Charley replied.   The boys each dug their spurs in and headed for Del Rio.

As they approached the edge of the town, they heard a gunshot ring past their heads.

"Holy shit!   Why's somebody shootin' at us in town?" Charley asked.

"I don't know, but I ain't going to wait around to find out either," Mario answered.

The shot came from a couple more of Pete O'Reilly's men that he had strategically placed waiting on the boys.   O'Reilly didn't expect them to be bold enough to ride out to the ranch and confront him face to face.   He figured he could send a couple to town to take care of business.   The boys headed northeast out of town.   They were headed for the Western Texas Hill Country.   They were about to find themselves fugitives, not from the law, but from Pete O'Reilly.

Zeke and Sam Keller, Together Again

After a few more weeks of hard traveling and following the Pedernales River as far as it would take them, the McDaniels wound up in Edwards County, Texas, one of the wildest and most unsettled parts of Texas.

"Are we there yet?" Thomas asked his father.

"'Pert near, son.   Old Sam told me his ranch was in Edwards County.   I believe that's where we are now," Ezequiel said.

"I hope so, Paw, my old backside can't take much more of this ridin', especially through all these hills and valleys Texas has," Tom told his dad.

Zeke chuckled a little bit as he saw a small German style farmhouse up in the distance.   "Well, we can stop there fer a spell and ask them folks if they know Sam Keller."

A few minutes later the McDaniels and their wagon rolled up to the front of the small farm.   An old farmer met them at the front door.

"Howdy," the old man said in a very thick German accent.

"Howdy," Zeke replied.   "My name is Ezequiel McDaniel.   I come from Alabama way, and I'm lookin' fer a feller by the name of Samuel Keller.   He's a rancher hereabouts in these parts."

"You mean to tell me you rode in that old wagon with those old tired mules half way across this country just to see Samuel Keller," the old German said.

For a minute Zeke really had to stare down the old man to see if he was serious or not.   He wasn't quite sure if the man thought of Sam as a friend or scoundrel.   About that time a smile broke out over the face of the old German.

"Yes, yes, I do know Sam Keller; he is a pretty good man, only because he is German like me, not a Scotsman like you!"   The old man broke out into a huge belly laugh.   "I'm only kidding, my friend.   Yes, old Sam lives about eight miles down this road.   It dead ends into his ranch.   He has one of the larger spreads in this part of the country.   You say he is an old friend of yours?"

"Yes, sir, we served in the war together.   I was with an Alabama militia, and he was with a Texas Calvary unit; but towards the end of that damn war the South was making patchwork units like grandma makes patchwork quilts," Zeke said with a big grin.   "Well, sir, we shore 'preciate the help.   If it's only eight more miles, we'll push on."

"Well, God ride with you, sir, you and your family," the old German told them.

After they passed the next eight miles, they rode up on the front gate of Sam's ranch.   It was still pretty early in the afternoon when they arrived. They rode on into the main ranch house.   Sam was looking out the window of his house, confused about why a wagon full of sodbusters was riding up his driveway.   At first, he didn't recognize Zeke and, of course, he didn't know his family or Marcus.

When they got to the house Zeke hollered, "Hello, the house."

Sam looked hard at who was crawling down off the wagon.   "Well, God almighty, I…will…be…a …suck…egg…mule!!   Zeke McDaniel, is that you?" Sam asked.

"It's me, you silly ass Texas sidewinder.   I done come to see ya."

Sam hopped down off the front porch like a young kid and Zeke did the same off the wagon.   They ran up and hugged each other like the long lost friends that they were.

"What in the hell are you doin' in Texas, boy?"   Sam asked his old pal.

"Well, hellfire, after listenin' to you go on and on 'bout all them cows runnin' loose here in Texas, I figured I'd try my hand at cowboying."

Sam invited everyone into the house, even Marcus.   One thing about old cowboys, they usually weren't as racist as some other folks were.   Besides the Mexicans had taught the whites all they knew about cows and horses. Out in the West all they cared about was, could the man do the job or not.

Later that night as they were having their dinner, Zeke explained the real reason they came west from Alabama.   He explained about how so many farms and farmland had been destroyed by the war.   He also told him about his son Jake getting sick and dying.   They just figured there was nothing left and it was time to start over.

"Damn, Zeke, I shore am sorry to hear about that boy of yorn.   I remember how you used to brag on 'em.   And this young feller here looks like he could make one hell of a cowboy," Sam said as he patted young Tom on the shoulder.

"Yeah, I tell ya, Zeke, that don't surprise me at all 'bout that lands being in bad shape.   God forgive us all, we shore did blow it all to hell!   Five damn years of killin' and it seems all we did was ruin a bunch of good farmland and bloody up lots of good waterin' holes.   Now I hear tell the damn Yankees done moved in anyway and took over the whole shebang.

"I tell ya what though, you damn shore made a good decision, comin' out here.   I wasn't feeding ya a line of bull.   It really is some damn fine country and there is plenty of cattle all around.

"I guess the biggest problem I've got nowadays, other than the beef market bein' bottomed out, is a feller on the far backside of my ranch.   A feller name of Pete O'Reilly, a damned old Irishman that moved down here a few years before the war started.   I got about 6,000 acres on my ranch.   And that old boy's probably got close to 12 or 15,000 over yonder east of Del Rio.   That's a little town there on the Rio Grande on the Mexican border.

"There's a pretty good strip of land there 'twixt the two ranches.   I'd like to buy it, but like I said with cattle prices what they are right now, I ain't got no money.   I'm gonna have to drive me a herd up to Missouri or Kansas to the rail heads next year.   Now that old Irishman could care less about buying it. He'll acquire it any damn way he can get his grubby little hands on it.

"I don't mind sharing it, hell it's all pretty much open range round these parts.   'Bout the only fences you'll see 'round here are ones around little old ladies' gardens.   But hells bells, ever time me or one of my hired hands is ridin' on that side of the ranch lookin' fer strays, them sons a bitches starts shootin' at us like they already own it.   Not to mention, more than one of my steers, with my brand, the Crooked S, has disappeared off the backside of this place.

"They's probably about 2,000 acres between our ranches.   It's good country, real perty, lots of small spring fed creeks and waterin' holes on it and lots of good grass.   Y'all could make a damn fine place out of it if you was a mind to.   I'll swan, Ezequiel, I'd shore rather have y'all fer neighbors than that son of a bitch that's over there right now."

Zeke nodded his head in agreement and pondered what his old friend had been telling him.   Later that night Zeke and Elizabeth lay in bed and talked about what Sam had told them.

"Well, honey, what do you think?" Elizabeth asked her husband.

"I don't know, darlin'," Zeke answered, staring at the ceiling, "We damn shore ain't turnin' back. We've done come too far and dealt with too much to even think about turnin' around and high tailin' it back to Alabama. I don't know anybody else here in this state. I figure we's just as good off here as striking out anywhere else."

"What about your nephew Charley and your brother-in-law Henry? They came to Texas years ago," Elizabeth said.

"Yeah, but I don't have a clue where they're at. Somewhere way out in West Texas, last time I heard. I wish I did know where they were at. I miss old Henry and I'd shore like to see that boy again too. I 'magine he's all growed up and haired over by now. Old Henry just lit out after sis passed on, he just couldn't handle it. After a few letters here and there we just lost touch."

Elizabeth nodded her head as she too stared at the ceiling. "Sounds like a barrel full of trouble here in this country, but I'm tired of runnin', Zeke, I want a home. I don't mind fightin' for it. I hope that war hadn't taken all the fight out of you."

Zeke laughed, "Nah, not by a damn sight. I still got plenty of fight left, plus I don't like the idea of some Irishman takin' potshots at my best friend. That settles it, darlin'. If you'll stand by my side, we'll stay and make a home here," Zeke told Elizabeth.

The next morning, the smell of coffee and bacon awakened the household. Sam had an old Mexican lady do most of his cooking for him at the house. She could make boot leather taste like T-bone steak.

"Howdy, Howdy......how you old sodbusters doin' this morning?" Sam asked as he flashed a big grin out from under that big handlebar mustache.

"Hell, we's finer than frog hair and twice as scarce!" Zeke answered as he took a hot cup of coffee from the old Mexican lady.

"Well, all right, y'all sit yourselves down and let's eat," Sam replied.

As they ate breakfast Zeke told Sam what he and Elizabeth had decided last night. He told him that they had decided to stay and try to make a home here. He told Sam that he would like to ride out and see the land that is for sale.

He told Sam he couldn't buy it all at once but he did have enough saved away to at least put a down payment on the land. Sam asked Zeke if he was really sure if he wanted to get tangled up in this range war. Zeke said he was, and Elizabeth was sure she wanted to do it too.   Zeke said he would offer Marcus the chance to leave if he wanted to.

About that time Marcus came in from outside.   "Where you been Marcus?" Zeke asked.

"Ah, I's jist out 'chonder checking on the stock, makin' shore everything's good," Marcus replied.

"Marcus, I got a question for ya.   We decided to try and buy that land on the backside of Sam's ranch.   Now, they's been lots of trouble out there. Sam said he's shot it out more than once with the old boy that owns the ranch on the other side of his.   I know you've had a hell of a hard trip yourself, so what I'm tryin' to tell ya is you can break off from here and go yer own way if you don't want to get mixed up in this range war."

"Mr. Zeke, I done told you time and time again.   I feels like y'all is my family.   I ain't got no other place to go.   If this is where y'all want to be, then this is where I wants to be!   You just give me a rifle and point me in the right direction!"   Marcus said and flashed a big old smile back to Zeke.

Zeke dropped his head and began to laugh.

Old Sam walked up behind Marcus and slapped him on the back and told Zeke, "Damn, Zeke, sounds like you got a fighter on your hands here!"

After breakfast Sam, Zeke and Marcus rode out across Sam's ranch towards the back side where the land was for sale.   Elizabeth and Tom stayed at the house and were told not to expect them back for a few days.   It would take a couple of days to get all the way across the ranch and they would probably scout it out a little once they get there.

Elizabeth agreed to stay at the ranch house and wait for them to return. She told them to be careful and make sure they had enough supplies packed with them.   She and Tom stood on the back porch of the house and waved as the men rode into the western horizon.

"Boy howdy, this is damn shore some nice country Sam," Zeke said.

"Yeah, it's amazing how nice land is when you don't blow it all to hell." The men all chuckled a little bit.   "Nah, the truth is, Zeke, it's a little piece of heaven out here.   The Indians ain't too bad.   We get along with the Mexicans just fine and there ain't hardly any nesters 'round here . . .   just lots of wide open country, just like God planned it."

"Is that some of your cows down there?" Zeke asked.

Sam took a long hard look down into a box canyon. "Nah, I don't believe so, that's some of them wild cows I used to tell you about. They's plenty more where they came from. They's also some mustangs running round these hills if you ever feel up to breakin' some of them."

"Damn, looks like the good Lord just supplied everything a man would need to get by out here," Zeke said.

Marcus nodded his head in agreement and said, "It shore do, Mr. Zeke, I do believe God spent a little more time makin' this country!"

"Yeah, 'bout the only thing we could use a little more of is some rain. Sometimes it comes down in bucketfuls, and then sometimes you won't see any after March.

The men continued riding and talking as they continued to chase that western sunset. Zeke and Marcus were extremely impressed with Sam's ranch and the type of land that was available in this part of Texas. They also noticed that they didn't see just wild livestock, but there was also plenty of wild game. The deer were plentiful not to mention turkeys, rabbits, squirrels, dove, and quail. Mid-afternoon of the second day they rode up to the back property line of Sam's ranch.

"Well, Zeke, there she be," Sam said.

Zeke and Marcus looked over the landscape. "Yeah, that's a mighty fine piece of land Sam, I could see why you'd want it."

"Yeah, lots of bullets have flew back and forth out here. I'd like to have it but I damn shore don't want to get shot over it," Sam said. While Sam was looking over the land, he noticed a rider on a hilltop on the other side. "Get down, ride over behind that thicket over there, and stay low."

Zeke and Marcus saw the rider that Sam had seen. So they rode down behind the little thicket so they would be out of sight.

"That's one of Pete O'Reilly's riders right there. I don't know his name but I've seen him around here before," Sam said. "I'll tell you another thing; where there's one of them boys, there's usually a few more not too far down the trail."

"We are still on my property here so let's just ease on back here. I ain't ready to tangle with them boys today," Sam told Zeke and Marcus.

"Yeah, I hear ya, I ain't ready to tangle just yet myself," Zeke said.

The men rode quietly back; a couple of miles into Sam's property.

"I tell ya what, fellers, we'll make camp here tonight and then we'll scout out a little more and see what we can see," Sam said.

Sam, Zeke, and Marcus set up camp for the night. Marcus built a fire while Sam shot a couple of rabbits for dinner and Zeke unsaddled and hobbled the horses for the night.

When Sam returned with the rabbits, Marcus had a pot of coffee boiling on the fire and Zeke was checking and cleaning his pistols.

"Hell, I figured I got my fill of fighting back in that damn war!" Zeke told Sam.

Sam smiled a little, "Yeah, I used to think the same thing 'til I got back to this ranch a couple of years ago. Seems anywhere I go these days I wind up shootin' at somebody. I don't want to………but it always seems somebody's pullin' a gun."

"Here ya go, Mr. Sam, let me have them rabbits, and I'll get 'em on the fire," Marcus told Sam.

Marcus took the rabbits from Sam's hand and cut a small hole in all of them then quickly jerked the hides off of them. A few minutes later he had them cut up and washed off. After a little dousing in some salt and pepper, the rabbits were frying away on the fire.

After the food was cooked, they ate up and washed it down with some hot coffee and a couple of shots of Tennessee sour mash. They stretched out on their bedrolls, taking turns looking up at the stars and having conversations about the future.

"You sure this is all worth it?" Sam asked.

Zeke continued to stare off into the distance; he nodded his head up and down while taking a sip of his coffee. "Yeah Sam, it's like I told you the other day. I didn't come all this way just to turn tail and run. I'm looking to start over, and by God, I like this Texas Country."

Sam had a sly grin come over his face and Marcus began to chuckle in approval. The men continued to visit as well as discuss how they were going to go about fighting Pete O'Reilly and his men for that land.

"Well, Ezequiel, if you got any ideas on how to take them boys down, I'd shore like to hear 'em," Sam said.

"Well, I got a brother-in-law and nephew that live farther west of here, maybe they could throw in with us. What kind of law y'all got out here?"

"None to speak of.   We got some Rangers that ride through from time to time, but you never know when they'll be here.   Folks 'round here pretty much do their own law enforcing."

"Yeah, that's kind of what I figured," Zeke answered.

"Well, the three of us and your brother-in-law and his boy makes five.   I can talk to some of my cowboys and see if they'd be willing to throw in.   I ain't gonna force 'em to do it," Sam said.

"Yeah, I agree there ain't no point in forcin' them to get involved in something that don't really concern 'em," Zeke told Sam.

"Well, if we ride hard tomorrow, we should be able to get back to the ranch. After that, I'll talk to the boys and see if they want in on this or not.   You can ride on and look for your brother in law and his son.   We got plenty of room to put your family up while you're gone.   When you get back with or without them we'll ride out to O'Reilly's ranch and get this thing started," Sam told Zeke.

"That sounds good, Sam, I'm obliged you would look after my family while I'm gone.   You know it might be a couple of weeks before I get back.   I hear it is still a pretty good ride out to the Presidio Country.   And, hell, they might not even be 'round there anymore.   But with or without 'em, y'all be ready to ride when I get back.   I'm ready to get this over with and settle down and build me a home," Zeke said.

The Reunion

When Sam, Zeke and Marcus made it back to the ranch, Zeke told Elizabeth what they had seen and what had happened. He told her how beautiful the land was on the backside of Sam's ranch, and how they saw one of Pete O'Reilly's boys out there riding the range. Instead of confronting him they pulled back and decided on a plan. The plan was that she, Tom, and Marcus would stay at Sam's ranch while he rode for Presidio and looked for Henry and Charley to see if they would be able to help them fight for this piece of land. Elizabeth wasn't too happy about it, but she agreed that it would be the right thing to do.

The next morning after breakfast, everyone went outside. Zeke began to pack his horse and load up all his possibels.

"You watch yourself, Ezequiel, I want you back here in one piece," Elizabeth told him.

"Don't worry, darlin', I made it through a war and came all this way. I reckon I'll be all right," Zeke answered with a smile. "Come here, boy," Zeke told Tom.

Tom ran over to his pa. Zeke reached down and gave him a big hug. "I love you son, and I promise you this will all be over soon enough and we will have us a new home."

Tom hugged his pa and held back a tear. Next Zeke shook Marcus's hand and told him how much he appreciated him sticking with his family through all of this. Sam came over and shook Zeke's hand.

"Don't you fret 'bout nothing, Zeke, your people will be fine here," Sam said.

"I know and I'm gonna hold you to it," Zeke told him.

The two men shook hands and Sam slapped him on the back. Zeke jumped up on his horse. As he gave his horse a kick he tipped his hat to everyone who was staying behind.

Zeke had a general idea of where Presidio was.   He knew it was west. But Sam had told him some general trails to follow that would help cut some time off his trip and make sure he gets there all right.   Zeke rode through sun, wind and even a couple of rare thunderstorms.

About two weeks after leaving the ranch Zeke arrived in Presidio.   Since he had no idea where Henry and Charley lived, he just rode into town and started to ask around.   He stopped off in the local saloon to drown some dust in his throat.   While he was in there he asked the bartender if he knew Henry or Charley.

"Howdy," the bartender said to Zeke as he nestled up to the bar.

"Howdy," Zeke said in return.

"What'll ya have, stranger?" the bartender asked.

"Well, after two weeks of swallowin' this West Texas dust, I'll take a double shot of bourbon and a beer chaser."

The bartender grinned as he threw his hand towel over his shoulder and turned around to fix the drinks.   As the bartender set up the drinks for Zeke he was asked about Henry and Charley.

"Henry Dalton? Hell, yeah, I know old Henry, hell of a good old boy, him and that boy of his . . .   big time horse traders round these parts.   I shore was sorry to hear what happened."

"What happened?" Zeke asked with a confused look on his face.

"Well, I can't say for damn shore, but the word around the campfire is he got killed down in Mexico.   Him and a couple of drifting cowboys lit out of here with a string of ponies a while back.   He ain't never come back.   Word came back that he got ambushed.   That boy of his, Charley, him and a Mexican boy, Mario, they went down there to see what happened," the bartender told Zeke.

Zeke slowly lowered his head and pushed his hat back.   He lifted his glass and took all the bourbon in one shot.   This one hit him pretty hard.   He always liked Henry and had been dreaming of living closer to him again so they could pick up where they left off when they were young men with new brides.

Zeke looked up at the bartender.   "Where 'bouts in Mexico was Henry headed?"

"Ain't too shore," the bartender replied. "He took out that way," the bartender pointed out the window in the general direction that Henry left.

"Much obliged," Zeke said as he finished his beer and stuck out his hand to thank him.

Zeke walked out of the bar and got on his horse and rode off. He had a combination of a heavy heart and a growing rage for his brother in law. Zeke stopped off just long enough to send off a letter back to Sam's ranch.

As he was on his way out of town he was stopped by Chente Suarez. "Señor, are you looking for Henry Dalton?"

Zeke looked down from his horse. "Yeah I am, why do you ask?"

Chente stuck his hand up and said. "My name is Vicente Suarez, but people call me Chente, and Henry was a good friend of mine. My son is riding with your nephew Charley. They went after the men that did this thing."

"Do you know where they went?" Zeke asked.

"No, Señor, I don't know, but I would like to go with you, señor. I am worried about Mario and Charley, not to mention I want to get the man who killed my friend."

"Well I don't know, friend, this thing might get rough and I don't want to be responsible for anybody else getting hurt," Zeke said.

"Don't worry about me. If I don't go with you I will just go out by myself," Chente answered.

Zeke nodded his head in reluctant agreement. Then he began to realize that Chente probably knew this country like the back of his hand and Zeke barely knew the directions. Also, it wouldn't hurt to have someone around that could speak Spanish, that was sure to come in handy out here.

"Where's yer stuff at?"

"My house is about three miles out of town in the same direction you were going," Chente answered. Chente mounted his horse and the two men rode out of town towards his home. When they arrived they dismounted and went inside.

"Antonia, donde estas?" Chente asked his wife. Antonia walked from around the corner. Chente introduced his wife to Zeke. Zeke took his hat off and shook her hand.

"Antonia, this is Mr. Zeke McDaniel," Chente said. "He is the brother in law of Henry."

Antonia was surprised but then collected herself and said, "Welcome to our home.   It is so nice to meet some of Henry's family; I am very pleased to meet you."

Chente then told her that he was packing up and going with Zeke.   She was understandably upset.   She began to argue with him in Spanish. Chente was trying to avoid an argument with her but hell hath no fury like a Mexican woman scorned.   Chente was walking around in the bedroom trying to pack his belongings while Antonia was one step behind him trying to talk him out of the whole idea.   While all this was going on Zeke was sitting in the kitchen at the table trying to act like he couldn't hear and see what was going on.

The arguing went on for about five minutes when finally Antonia gave up. Antonia was not pleased with his decision, but she knew it was foolish to try and talk him out of it.   She began to help him pack the things he would need for the trip.   While she was doing that Chente was getting his guns ready. He grabbed his rifle and pistol belt as well as plenty of ammunition.   After everything was gathered and packed, Chente kissed his wife goodbye.   She told them to be careful and bring the boys back home safely.   Chente and Zeke rode off and crossed the river into Mexico.   Zeke started to realize what a smart move it was to bring Chente with him.   Not only did he know the lay of the land but he also spoke the language which would be invaluable where they were going.   Not to mention you can never have too many guns on your side.

The first night they made camp and got a little better acquainted.   Zeke told Chente all about the trip from Alabama.   He told about all the hardships they had faced along the way.   He told him about the death of his son and how that pretty much was the last straw on staying back in the old South.

"Señor, I have never been east of San Antonio, but I understand there was a lot of damage done in that part of the world," Chente said.

"Yeah, it was pretty bad.   Back before the war I had me a pretty good farm.   It wasn't one of them plantations like you hear about, but it was still a pretty nice place and it was all mine.   It would grow anything I had a mind to grow.   I also ran me a few head of good stock, too. We had plenty of rain, plenty of sunshine, lots of good growing weather, lots of good friends, and credit down at the bank and grocery store.   But that's all changed now I guess.   Half the people I knew are either dead or mangled."

"The more stories I hear about that war, I thank God that I lived so far away from it.   We would hear stories but it might as well have been on the other side of the world," Chente replied.

Chente also told Zeke stories about Henry and Charley.   He told him about when he first came out West and how Chente took him under his belt and taught him about cowboying and ranching.   He told him how Charley spent as much time at his house as he did at his own house, and how Antonia was sort of a surrogate mother to Charley.   Charley and Mario pretty much grew up together as close as brothers.

"Henry was a good man and a good friend.   I don't think he knew how to take me when we first met.   It was obvious that he had never worked for a Mexican before," Chente said.

Zeke just laughed.   "Yeah, I bet that was a shock to the old system for Henry."

"He worked very hard, though.   He was determined to make a life out here for him and his son.   You could tell early on.   He was not going to let anything stop him.   He had come too far trying to run away from the ghost of his wife," Chente said.

"Yeah, I reckon I know how he was feeling on that one.   You just keep running and running trying to leave those ghosts as far behind as you can.   Then one day you realize, you don't want to forget them.   You just don't want to hurt so much when you think about them," Zeke said.

One good night of talking bridged the gap of a lot of years that were missed.   Zeke and Chente felt like they had known each other for years because of their connections to Henry and Charley.

The next morning Chente and Zeke finished breakfast and sucked down the last cup of coffee.   After burying the fire they saddled up and set out on the trail again.   A couple of days later they arrived in the same little village where Charley had gone to find out about his father after he buried him.

When they rode into town Zeke looked at Chente and said, "I'll ask the questions, but you do the talking."

Chente laughed a little and agreed.   They walked into a little cantina and sat down at the bar.   Chente ordered two tequilas and two beers.   As the bartender was bringing the drinks, Zeke made eye contact with a couple of vaqueros and asked about Henry.   Chente then told them what he said in Spanish.

The two vaqueros looked at each other and then just walked out of the bar. Zeke started to holler at them but Chente put his hand on Zeke's shoulder and quietly said to let them go.   Zeke turned around to the bar and slammed his shot of tequila and then started in on the beer.

About that time a man walked up to the bar, never looked at them, but started talking in a low voice.   The man could speak English, and he told them what had happened.   He told them that a few weeks ago two men who were working with Henry jumped him outside of town.   He told them that two young men, a Mexican and a Gringo, rode into the town also asking about it.   Zeke told him that that was his nephew and his friend's son.   The man at the bar had been there the day they rode in and heard about it.   He told them everything that he knew.   He didn't have a dog in this fight but what had happened upset a lot of people in the village.

"Señor, the men you are looking for are from Del Rio.   I hear they work for a rich Gringo named Peter O'Reilly.   He is supposed to be a horse trader and cattle rancher.   I think maybe he wanted your brother-in-law's horses.   If you are looking for those two boys that came through here, I would go to Del Rio. That is probably where you will find them."

The men finished their drink and thanked the man for his help.   They saddled up and rode out of town.   They were both hell bent for Del Rio.   It took almost a week to get there, but finally, they arrived a few miles out of town on the Mexican side of town.

Zeke decided to sneak into town and ask around.   Purely by chance, he went to the livery stable just like Charley had when he was looking for answers.   Zeke stepped into the back door of the barn and made his way towards the front.   He looked out the door and saw Old Bill working on some horseshoes.

"Howdy," he said.

Old Bill nearly jumped out of his skin, "Great gobs of goat tracks!" he screamed as he put his hand over his heart.   "I'll Swan, mister, don't you know better than to come up on a man with a hot horseshoe in his hand; I could've charred my pod."

"Sorry, partner, didn't mean to scare you or your pod.   I was hoping you could help me out.   I just rode into town and I'm looking for a couple of boys in their early twenties, a Mexican and a white feller, may of rode through here."

"Yeah, I know them boys," answered Bill.   "You just missed them boys by a few days or so.   They went riding out to old Pete O'Reilly's ranch hell bent for leather.   They was gonna shoot it out with Pete and his boys. Trying to get a little revenge for what they done to that boy's paw. You happen to know them boys?" Old Bill asked.

"Yeah, that's my nephew, and that Mexican boy with him is a family friend. And his paw was my brother in law.......God Dammit," Zeke said with a sigh and sound of depression.

"Well, last I heard them boys was still alive.   They said there was a lot of shootin' out at O'Reilly's ranch.   Them boys rode back into town and some cowboys started shooting at them down here too.   Last I saw 'em they sunk spur and headed northeast out of town trying to stay ahead of that posse," Bill told Zeke.

"You say they was headed northeast?" Zeke asked.

"Yessir, they lit a shuck headed that way," as Bill pointed in the general direction of Sam's ranch.

Zeke stuck his hand out to Old Bill and said, "Much obliged."

Bill shook Zeke's hand and wished him the best of luck on what he had to do.

Zeke met up with Chente to tell him what he had found out at the livery stable.   He told him that the boys had been there and already went after the man that killed Henry but then they had to take off again because now they were being chased.

"Well, Zeke, what do you want to do now, my friend?" Chente asked.

"Well, we ain't got a hell of a lot to go on but I reckon we're gonna have to ride northeast and see what we come across," he answered.

Zeke and Chente rode out of town heading into the far western end of the Texas Hill Country.   They had no idea where to find the boys; they were just hoping for a good clue or a hot trail.   They pushed their horses pretty hard and made a little over 30 miles in two days.   They still hadn't had any luck. They continued to press on; they were determined to find the boys come hell or high water.   But in West Texas, it's usually just hell.

On the third day they rode up on a small run down plank wall cabin with an old man sitting on the porch.   He had a jug in one hand and a double-barreled "greener" on his lap.

"That'll be far enough gents," the old man said in a calm undisturbed voice. "Just what is it I can do for you fellers?"

Just as Zeke started to tell the old man who they were and what they wanted, Charley stepped out from behind the cabin with his rifle drawing a dead bead on Zeke.

"I don't know what they want but I'll tell you what they're gonna get and that's a one way ticket to Hell," Charley yelled.

Charley automatically assumed that the men were some of Pete O'Reilly's men. He didn't recognize Chente right off because he was riding a little behind Zeke, and he had his handkerchief over his face trying to keep out some West Texas dust that had been blowing, which made them look even more like bad men. Charley didn't recognize Zeke either because of being gone for so many years.

"Whoa, Carlitos, don't shoot, mijo!" exclaimed Chente. "It's me, Chente, I am here with your tio, Zeke, from Alabama."

Charley stopped, and looked closer, he now obviously recognized Chente but he stared really hard at his Uncle. "Uncle Ezequiel, God Damn, is that you?"

"Yeah, boy, it's me, you wanna set that hammer down easy on that old pea shooter?"

Charley stared in disbelief; not only had he not seen his uncle in forever, this was the last place on the planet he expected to see him or any other kin. Charley slowly set the hammer back down on the rifle as he lowered it down to his hips. He stood there still not believing what he was seeing.

"Uncle, what in the Hell are you doing in West Texas?" Charley said, still not believing what he was seeing.

"I came to Texas for my family; I came here to find you," Zeke said in a matter of fact voice.

Zeke and Chente slowly and gingerly got off their horses. As they made their way over to Charley, he rushed over and gave each one of them a huge hug. Partly because he hadn't seen his uncle in so many years and partly because, after coming so close to dying, there were not two other men he would rather see.

"Mijo, donde esta Mario?" Chente asked Charley.

"Ah, don't fret none, Chente, he's all right. This old timer on the porch here said we was welcome to hold up here for a while as long as we brought our own food, so Mario lit out this morning looking for a deer or hog or something. He'll be along pretty soon. God Almighty, it's good to see y'all again," Charley said as he hugged each one of them again.

The old man on the porch laughed a little and then pushed his hat back and scratched his old gray head. "Well, I reckon we's gonna have a few more for supper this evening."

Everybody kinda chuckled and they all walked into the cabin.

The next few hours were spent catching up on all the years that had passed by. Zeke told Charley about the war and what happened to the farm and to his cousin Jake. He told him how much he was looking forward to living closer to his brother-in-law and starting a new life. Charley told Zeke what it was like growing up in West Texas and living right next to Mexico.

About that time the cabin door swung open. Mario had returned.

"Papi, what the hell are you doing here?" Mario exclaimed.

"I came with this man, this is El Tio de Charley," Chente answered.

Zeke stood up from the table and introduced himself, "Howdy, son, you must be Mario. I've heard a lot of good things about you."

Mario came in and shook Zeke's hand. "How do you do sir, it is nice to meet you."

"Ah, hell, boy you ain't got to call me sir. From what I hear you and old Charley are close as brothers, you just call me Zeke."

Mario smiled and said, "Ok, Zeke, nice to meet you."

The old man looked up from the table and said, "Well, son, what's for dinner?"

"It's out there on my horse, Viejo," Mario replied with a grin.

"Well, I tell you what, you fellers stay in here and get better acquainted and I'll tend to dinner."

As the old man got up to go outside Zeke said, "Well, boys, I guess we better get to the rat killing, Lord knows we didn't all ride out this far just fun."

Charley nodded his head and said, "You damn shore got that right, Uncle! Uncle Zeke, how in the hell did you find me way out here?" he asked.

"Well, boy, like I said, we decided to move out west hoping to find you and your pa. I set out to find him and some folks told me what happened so I did the same thing you did. I went after the men who did it. There's more to it than that though. My friend Sam is having some trouble on his place too with O'Reilly. Seems they're disputing where the property line is on the back side of his place. I am trying to buy some land out there myself, but there ain't never gonna be no peace with a man like that around..."

"Yeah, Unc, you got that right, but I guarundamntee you there will be justice," Charley said in a dead set voice.

"Oh yeah, there will be justice boy, don't you fret none about that. But we gonna have to be smarter and stronger to beat that Irish son of a bitch," Zeke replied.

"What'chu got in mind, Unc?" Charley asked.

"We gonna lay low here tonight, eat up, rest and then we'll head back to Sam's spread in the morning. We'll all throw in with him and his boys and then we'll finish this thing once and for all," Zeke replied.

Calm Before The Storm

The next morning before the sun ever thought about breaking the night sky, Zeke and the others were awakened by the smell of coffee and bacon. Zeke rose up from his bedroll and scratched his sides through his long johns while he let out a huge yawn.

The old man looked over at him and said, "Morning."

"Morning," Zeke replied.

"I know what you boys have got to do and I know what y'all are up against. That son of a bitch O'Reilly has run roughshod over me, too, in the past. I know I ain't no match for him but just maybe you fellers are. You got a long ride ahead of ya and a man can't ride good on an empty stomach. So you boys get up and get over here and get fed. It's the least I could do for the fellers going up against him."

"You say you had a run in with O'Reilly, too?" Zeke asked.

"Yeah, I guess it was nigh on four years ago I had a small place. It wadn't huge but by God, it was mine. I had me about 120 acres in this little valley between two big old hills. O'Reilly came by and tried to buy me out. I told him I wadn't interested. He kept on and kept on and just wouldn't quit. Finally, he showed up with a couple of his boys one day and before they even got to my front door I gave 'em a couple barrels of buckshot. Ha! Their damned old horses reared up and they commenced to fighting 'em. They finally got them horses calmed down and turned around and lit out.

"But that wasn't the end of it, though. A few days later I got up to do my morning chores. I got out to the barn and every one of my animals was graveyard dead."

"Dead!" Zeke exclaimed.

"Yes sir, someone had snuck into my farm and poisoned all my hogs, goats, chickens and horses. I reckon they put some kind of poison in their troughs overnight. I saddled up and rode out through the pastures to check on my cows.   I was runnin' about 30 head.   I rode all over my 120 acres and didn't see hide nor hair of any of them.   I reckon O'Reilly's boys must have rustled 'em off.

"Now if that don't beat all, while I was out lookin' fer my cows, they rode up to my cabin and burned the whole place down.   When I got back there wadn't nothing left but ashes. This place I got now was given to me by an old rancher friend of mine.   He cut out two acres here for me and helped me put up this little cabin.   I guess it's enough to get by on.   I got me a couple hogs and few chickens.   That along with a few catfish and deer meat I get by okay."

"Well, we shore do appreciate it, partner," Charley said as he sat up in his bedroll.   "You know what, I been here a couple of days now and I never did catch your name."

"Names don't count for much out here."   The men all kind of looked at each other, a little puzzled but none of them pressed the old man about it. "Viejo" and "old timer" seemed to be good enough names for him.   He had been a good host to them and that seemed to be enough.

After all the men stuffed their gut with bacon, biscuits and some real strong coffee, they went outside and each started to saddle up.   The very first sign of an early morning sun was turning the night sky the slightest bit orange. Each man took his turn shaking the old man's hand and telling him how much they appreciated the hospitality.

He smiled back and said, "Y'all just git that son of a suck egg mule!"

They all started back towards Sam's ranch.   It would still take a couple days riding to get there.   They had good luck in that they didn't see any Comanches, actually, no Comanches saw them.   They also had no run-ins with Pete O'Reilly's men.   They just rode and camped and rode and camped until they reached Sam's place. A few days after leaving the old man's cabin they crossed Sam's land and got back to the ranch house.

"Anybody home?" Zeke yelled as they approached the house.

"Zeke!" Elizabeth yelled as she came running out of the house, off the porch and across the yard.

About the same time, Sam stepped out of his barn and looked to see all the men riding up.   He made his way over to them and said "Well, I see you boys still have your hair."

"Yeah we didn't see nary an Indian out there but we did have some run-ins," Zeke said.   As Zeke dismounted his horse he started to introduce everyone.

"Elizabeth, this is your nephew Charley," Zeke said.   Elizabeth looked into Charley's eyes and started to cry.   "Oh my God, Charley, you've gotten so big, look at the man you've grown into."   Elizabeth lunged towards Charley and hugged him like he hadn't been hugged in years.   It was a long genuine show of affection from a family member he hadn't seen since he was a small boy.   It reminded him of the love and affection his own mother used to show him.   He hugged her back tightly and for just a moment felt like a small boy again without a worry in the world.

When she let go of him she stepped back and wiped tears from her eyes.   A little embarrassed, Charley wiped a small tear from his eye, too, without trying to be too obvious about it.   Elizabeth then reached out and gave a big hug to Zeke.

Zeke then said, "Elizabeth this is Vicente 'Chente' Suarez.   Did I say that right?"

Chente laughed a little and said, "Si, you said it right.   How do you do Mrs. McDaniel?   It is an honor to make your acquaintance.   May I introduce my son Mariano Suarez, everyone calls him Mario."

"My, I have heard about dashing, gallant Mexican gentleman, now I see it with my own eyes!" Elizabeth said as she reached out her hand to meet Mario.

"It is a pleasure to meet you, Mrs. McDaniel, we are always happy to meet family of Carlitos," Mario said as he removed his hat and kissed her hand.

"I'm sorry…Carlitos…?"   Elizabeth said with a confused voice.

"Charley, ma'am, that's how we say Charley in Spanish," Chente told her.

"Well, y'all don't just stand out here like you had good sense, let's go in the house and get comfortable and tell us all about it," said Sam.   Soon everyone made their way into the house and settled in on the chairs and couches in the parlor and began to discuss what had happened.

Zeke explained how he was on a long search for Henry.   When he learned of Henry's death he set out to find Charley.   He and Chente teamed up and rode down into Mexico.   Finally, they were in a wild goose chase back to Del Rio to find both the boys.   It looks like, as fate would have it, everybody's got the same enemy now.   They believed Pete O'Reilly was responsible for Henry's death as well as the range war on the back end of Sam's ranch.

Zeke was doubly furious now.   It was bad enough that O'Reilly caused this range war with his friend but he was also responsible for the death of his brother in law.   He knew this was going to end in a bloody mess but he also was determined to come out on top of this.

There was now a silence over the room, everyone was looking down at the floor or staring somewhere off in space.   Everyone was trying to think of what to do next.   The next minute or two felt like an eternity.

Finally Sam broke the ice and said, "Well, folks, what are we gonna do about this situation we got?"

Charley was the first to reply, "Kill 'em, kill every one of them bastards."

Zeke knew Charley was speaking from the heart but he also knew he was being a little hot headed about the whole thing.   If they were going to live through this whole thing and make a life for themselves, this was going to have to be thought through a little more thoroughly.

"I know where you're coming from boy; I feel the same way you do.   But we gonna have to be sensible if we gonna make it through this thing alive," Zeke told Charley.

Charley knew his uncle was probably right but he didn't really want to hear about it right then.   He really hadn't had the time to grieve for the loss of his father and put all his affairs in order back in Presidio.   He had pretty much been living off rage for the last couple of weeks.   That's a powerful high but it burns out quickly and he was just now coming down off of it.

Zeke looked around the room and said, "We got six guns here between the men folk.   How many you reckon O'Reilly has?"

Sam answered back, "What we got here is two wore out old soldiers, a field hand, a horse breeder and two Banty roosters.   O'Reilly's got at least 20 hired gunmen.   They may tend his cattle some but they're about as much of a cowboy as I am a dance hall girl.   They're mercenaries.   No families, no wife and kids back home cryin' for them."

Sam wasn't trying to sound insulting, he was just trying to drive home the point that those men had nothing to lose and they were only in it for the money.   His bunch, on the other hand, was not killers, they were farmers and ranchers and more importantly, they were family men.

This sort of back and forth went on for the better part of the evening. Everybody was coming up with ideas but they were just basically versions of the same plan.   It was all to load up and attack Pete O'Reilly's ranch.

Finally, among all the squabbling Marcus looked up and said something, "If y'all don't mind my sayin' so, it seems to me if you can't attack him from the front, maybe what y'all need is to attack him from the inside out."   Everybody else stopped talking for a minute and looked at Marcus.

"What are you getting' at, Marcus?"   Zeke asked.

"Well, a long time ago, my grandpappy used to tell me this story 'bout this old squirrel used to walk back and forth from his house to his favorite swimmin' hole each day.   He'd go down yonder, dive in and take him a swim to cool off from that hot Alabama sun!   'Til one day this old bobcat showed up in the middle of the road, yes sir, and he wadn't 'bout to let this squirrel pass on by.   No reason ya see, he was just a mean old cuss that like to hurt people.

"Every day Mr. Squirrel would try to sneak down that swimming hole and before he could make it, that old bobcat would pop out of nowhere and commence to layin' a whippin' on him.   Finally, Mr. Squirrel got so tired of it he decides he's gonna get him some revenge on that old bobcat.

"So he dresses himself up right perty like a female bobcat!   I know what you're thinkin' now, stay with me.   Well, sir, that old bobcat was fit to be tied, he let his guard down and started trying to sweet-talk that old lady bobcat. She got to earning his trust little by little 'til one day he says, 'why don't you come on over to my house'.   Mr. Squirrel agreed and they set out arm in arm back to old Mr. Bobcat's place.   They had themselves a good old time that night.

"The next mornin' they wake up and she says 'why you don't let me make you some breakfast'.   Well, that sounds real good to Mr. Bobcat so he lays up in bed while she commences to cookin'.   Ooh wee, it smells mighty fine.   But what Mr. Bobcat don't realize is…."

"She poisoned him," Chente broke in.   Everyone stopped listening to Marcus and looked over to Chente.   "Yes, I am very familiar with that story, my grandfather told a similar story except it was in Mexico and it was a rabbit and a fox.   But it is the same story.   The smaller, weaker animal gains the trust of the other one and then moves in for the kill when they get the opportunity."

"Yeah, that's about right," Marcus replied.   "I kinda figured if I moseyed on over to Mr. Pete's ranch and tell him I'm a newly freed slave lookin' fer some work, I might be able to get in there and raise a little hell, maybe see if I can even up the odds a little bit."

"Now just how do you plan on doin' that?" Zeke asked.

"Well, sir, I knows my way around the kitchen a little bit.   Maybe he be lookin' for a cook.   You know I can also handle horses and cattle, maybe I'll be one of these here cowboys!"   Marcus said with a sly grin on his face.

"I don't know, Marcus, I didn't bring you out all this way just to get you killed. I already damn near did that in Austin. You been too loyal and too good a man, I don't wanna get you hurt," Zeke told him.

"Well, you got any better idea?" Marcus asked him.

"You know the man has a point there, Ezequiel," said Sam. "If we could get us somebody in there on the inside it might make all the difference in the world."

Zeke continued thinking about what Marcus and Sam had said. He didn't like the idea but he was having a hard time coming up with a better idea. He knew it would be suicide to storm the place the way Charley and Mario did. They were lucky to get off that ranch alive. Still, he was having a hard time deciding what to do. He was running low on options. They knew this is where they wanted to stay. The land was beautiful, they already had friends, and the cattle were plentiful.

Finally, Elizabeth chimed in and broke the silence that hung over the room. "Well, y'all hash this out, and you better come up with something good. I'm gonna go start supper. Sam where is your cellar?"

Elizabeth got up and excused herself from the living room and the rest of the men. She went to the cellar and started to collect what she needed to feed everyone a big meal that night.

"Well, señores, have we come to a conclusion?" Chente asked.

Zeke looked across the room to Marcus and said, "All right, Marcus, we'll try it your way, but I'm gonna be awful mad at you if you get yourself strung up over there." Everyone kind of chuckled.

Marcus answered him with a big grin, "Don't you worry 'bout that none, Mr. Zeke, ain't nobody gonna be more upset than me if I gets myself strung up!" At that time everyone in the room burst into laughter and kind of let out a tension that had been present since they began to have this conversation on how to deal with Pete O'Reilly.

"All right, Marcus, what's your plan? How do you plan on pulling this thing off?" Zeke asked.

"Well like I said, I'll make my way over there, make up a name and tell him I needs a job. I'll tell him I can do most anything. If he need a cook, I'm his man. If he need somebody to wrangle them horses or feed his cows, I can perty much do it all. I figure if I can get in there and make a hand I'll be able to get to them and then I can starts to cut 'em down a bit."

Charley and Mario sat and listened intently. They both wanted to jump in and offer suggestions but they both realized they really didn't have any good ideas.   Besides after the stunt they pulled attacking O'Reilly head on, nobody really cared to hear their plans anyway.

"All right, Marcus, first light tomorrow you head down yonder to Pete's ranch and see what you can do.   Now I'm gonna tell ya right now; if he says no, don't push it.   If he ain't looking to hire, just tip yer hat and say thank ya, sir, and move on out.   The worst thing you can do is push it and either piss him off or worse, start to make him suspicious," Zeke told him.

"He is right, Marcus; I've heard about O'Reilly, and he is a cold-blooded killer.   Do what you can but the most important thing is to make sure you walk away alive," Chente added.

The men continued to hash out the details on how they were going to go on with the plan.

A little while later Elizabeth stuck her head back into the living room, "Dinner's ready, y'all come eat."

"Well, come on y'all, let's get some grub, a man can't think too good anyway on an empty stomach," Sam said as he stood up from his chair and slapped Chente and Mario on the back and guided them into the dining room.

The next half hour was pretty quiet as everyone dug into the meal that Elizabeth fixed.

Finally, Sam was the first to break the silence when he said, "Miss Elizabeth, that was mighty fine.   I got me a pretty good cook here but he can't hold a candle to you."

"Why thank you, Sam, it's always nice to be appreciated," she answered. Next Chente, Mario, and Charley seconded the motion.   "I'm sorry, I didn't have time to make no dessert, but I got plenty of coffee on the stove," she added.

Everybody added that was okay, they were too stuffed on beef steak, vegetables, and potatoes to have room for any pie or pudding.   "Tom, why don't you help me put away these dishes and let these menfolk talk a spell," she said.

"Okay, mama," replied Tom.   He really wanted to stay in there and listen to the men make their plan to get O'Reilly, but at the same time, he was smart enough not to get on his mom's bad side.

While Elizabeth and Tom put the dishes away and cleaned up, Sam reached into a cabinet and brought out a half-full bottle of Kentucky bourbon to freshen up everybody's coffee cup.   The men then pulled out what they had to smoke.   Some had pipes, others cigars, and a couple of roll-yer-owns.

The next couple of hours the men drank, smoked, and talked about what was about to happen and how they were going to deal with it.

"Well, boys, I reckon I had about all the fun I can stand.   I'm gonna hit the hay.   Elizabeth and Zeke got one spare bedroom; y'all can fight over the other.   The losers can fight over the floor, and I got some room cleared out and cleaned up in the hay loft in the barn so y'all just find you a place to bed down for the night," Sam told everyone.   The men all stood up and thanked Sam for his hospitality and shook hands for the night.   Chente took the spare bedroom.   Mario and Charley had planned on pitching a bedroll on the living room floor, but they noticed Marcus walking outside to the barn.

"Hey, Marcus, why don't you bed down in here tonight?" the boys asked.

"Naw, I reckon I best be stayin' out yonder in the barn."

Basically, it was a case of old habits die hard.   Sam had no problem letting Marcus sleep in the house, but it still didn't feel right to Marcus.   He realized there was going to take a lot of getting used to in this "free" world.

Mario and Charley looked at each other and said, "Well hell, if he's gonna sleep out in the barn, I guess it wouldn't hurt us none either."

They each grabbed their bedrolls and followed Marcus out to the barn. They caught up to him at the big double doors and patted him on the back. He just smiled and they all went inside, climbed up into the loft and bedded down for the night.

The next morning was a cool damp morning with an overcast sky.   Just as the first gray light was peering through the planks in the barn, Sam's rooster began to crow, waking Charley, Mario, and Marcus up.   Marcus rolled over and lit the lantern and moved it where it could shed light on everyone.

"Mornin' boys, how'd yall sleep last night?" he asked.

"Mighty fine, mighty fine Marcus," Charley answered.

Mario stood up and stretched out then started putting on his shirt.   "I smell food, sabes que? Tengo hambre," he said.   Marcus looked at him with a confused look on his face.

Charley looked at Marcus and laughed.

"He said he's hungry, Marcus," Charley said.

"Lord I didn't know I was gonna have to learn me a whole other language when I got to Texas.   I can't even talk English none too good!" Marcus said.

The boys laughed and finished getting dressed. They all made their way down to the ladder and out the barn. There was a pump and a trough between the barn and house and they all stopped over there to wash up and look presentable.

"Whoa, that's cold. That'll shore enough shrivel a man," Charley said. Mario laughed and splashed a little water back at him. Soon the three of them made their way back to the house and let themselves in.

"Morning, morning, anybody up," Charley asked?

"Y'all come on in this house," Sam replied as he walked up with a fresh brewed cup of hot coffee. "Ms. 'Lizbeth's in there cooking breakfast. Coffee's on the stove," Sam said.

The boys made their way into the kitchen where everyone else had gathered. "Morning boys. How'd y'all sleep last night?" Elizabeth asked while she scrambled the eggs.

"Not bad, Mrs. McDaniel, not bad at all," Mario said in a half yawning voice.

"Yeah, it did git a tad cool not long before the break of morning," Charley added.

"Yeah, there is a little frost on the pumpkin this morning, ain't there?" Sam added.

Soon breakfast was ready. It was a steaming plate of biscuits, gravy, good German cured bacon, and scrambled eggs with lots of coffee to spare. Everyone sat down. Elizabeth said grace and thanked the Lord for all he had provided and asked his protection for what she knew they had to do.

Here We Go

So it was agreed on by all what they were going to do. After breakfast, Elizabeth and Tom again put away the dishes and cleaned off the table while the men retried to the living room to put their plan into action.

"All right, Marcus, you ready to do this?" Zeke asked.

"Yes, sir, let's get on with it," Marcus replied.

"Okay, remember, as far as O'Reilly's concerned, you're just an ex-slave, poor as Job's turkey and lookin' fer some work. If he hires you on, you just kinda lay low and get used to the place. We're gonna need some kinda signal for you to let us know when you're ready."

"Well, what you want me to do, I can't read nor write, so's I can't send no letter. I can't very well go talk to y'all whenever I please," Marcus said with a slight hint of concern.

"I tell you what," Sam said. "At the end of the road leading out of O'Reilly's ranch, there's big old live oak tree on the right-hand side. You can't miss it. Anyhow, we'll ride by there once every few days to check on it. When you're ready you put two small rocks in the first fork of the tree on the north side. Maybe if he sends you to town or something, you can pass it and let us know. When we see it we'll take the rocks down so's you know, and we'll hit him the following morning."

"All right, Mr. Sam, that sounds like a plan," Marcus told him as he stuck out his hand to shake Sam's.

Everybody made their way outside to help Marcus pack his horse and get ready. He shook everybody's hands and they all wished him good luck and told him to be careful, especially Zeke who had grown especially fond and proud of Marcus.

Soon Marcus rode away towards Pete O'Reilly's ranch. No one knew what lay ahead but they all knew there was no turning back now. Everyone had a vested interest in this thing working out. Zeke wanted revenge for his brother in law and the land that was available. Sam wanted to put an end to this range war.   Charley also wanted revenge for his father's death and theft of horses.   Chente and Mario wanted to see justice for a man that killed a dear friend of theirs.

"Well, boys, there ain't no sense in standing around here just watchin' him ride off down the trail; we got guns to clean and ammo to gather up," Sam said, kind of stating the obvious.   "Zeke, what'chu got in the way of firearms?" Sam asked.

"Well, uh, I got a shotgun, .50 caliber Muzzleloader, and Colt Navy revolver," Zeke answered.

"Hellfire, man, that ain't gonna do us much good!" Sam answered in a half joking, half serious voice.   "Chente, what y'all got?" Sam asked.

"I have a Winchester '66 in my saddle; Mario should have one, too, in his. Plus we each have Walker .44s," Chente answered.

"Now yer talkin'," Sam said with a little more excitement in his voice. "Charley, what you carry, son?" Sam asked.

"I got a Henry and a Colt .44," Charley replied.

"All right, well that and what I got in the gun cabinet should be enough to arm us up pretty good when we go out there,"   Sam said.   "Git yer guns and let's go in the house and oil 'em up and see how we're sitting on ammo."

As they all walked back to the house, Sam put his arm around Chente and asked him, "Tell me something, Chente, where'd you get them two nice Winchesters?"

Chente grinned and looked at Sam and said, "Señor, you forget I am a horse trader, that's what I do!"   Sam let out a big old laugh and slapped him on the back as they made their way up the porch steps and into in the house.

The next couple of hours were spent collecting guns and cleaning and oiling them up, getting ready for the impending fight.   Sam dug through his gun cabinet and brought out all the boxes of .44 ammo he could find.   He made sure everyone would have two side arms and one long gun and all the ammo they could run with.   He knew, as did Zeke, that once the shooting started there was no turning back.

The next morning Marcus made his way to Pete OReilly's ranch.   He turned his horse at the big live oak tree that Sam was talking about.   Soon he rode past the main gate and came up to the house.   He reined in his horse, took a deep breath, swallowed hard and then dismounted.   He began walking up closer to the house with the reins in his hand.   He was looking around the front of the house for some sign of life.   Suddenly he heard a voice in a thick Irish accent from behind.

"Can I help you?" said Pete O'Reilly.

It caught Marcus off guard a little and he turned around and took his hat off and said, "Yes, sir, my name is Smitty, sir."   (Smitty was the first name that came to mind because it was the name of a good friend of his when he was a boy in Alabama.)   "I'm a freed slave, sir, I comes from Alabama.   They ain't no kinda life for a black man back there so I saddled up and headed west as soon as I could.   I was lookin' for some work, sir.   I'm honest and I works real hard, sir.   I can cook, clean, handle cattle and horses, farm anything you need, sir."

Pete was listening until the last line Marcus said.   "I am not a farmer, Mr. Smitty!"   Pete really took offense to the last thing Marcus said.   "Look around you, does this look like a farm?   Do you see fields of crops?   Do you see pigs, chickens and dairy cows? My father was a potato farmer in Ireland. He went broke doing it.   He became a drunkard over it and used to beat my mother and me because he was such a bad farmer.   You ignorant Nigger, do you not know the difference between a farm and a cattle ranch?"

Marcus was pretty flustered now.   "No, sir, I mean yes, sir, I knows the difference!"   He let out a little nervous laugh.   "I sho' do know the difference between a farm and ranch, yes, sir.   This sho' ain't no farm.   All I see is cows and some mighty fine horse stock."

"Do you know about horses, Mr. Smitty?"   Pete asked.

"Yes, sir, yes, sir uh, Tennessee Walkers, Quarter Horses, Thoroughbreds just about anything you wanna talk about," Marcus answered.   He was stretching the truth a little.   He was good with horses and knew about them, but he was not the expert he made himself to be.

Pete stared at Marcus, not sure what to make of this situation.   It was a little strange to have a black man show up in the West Texas Hill Country out of the blue and looking for a job.   "I don't know, why don't you come back tomorrow and we'll talk tomorrow?"   Pete said.

"Yes, sir, I sho' will," Marcus said.

Marcus was a little disappointed.   He only had a couple of dollars in his pocket and he knew he couldn't go back to Sam's ranch and risk being given away.   So he rode into the nearest town, or at least what passed for a town. As Marcus rode away, Pete called for one of his men and told him to follow Marcus to see what he was up to.

Marcus rode into the town and out of habit walked up to the back of a store and knocked on the door.   An older widow woman answered the door and asked him what he wanted.

"Scuse me, ma'am, I was just wonderin' if I could get me somethin' to eat for dinner.   I gots some money," Marcus said.

"Just wait here, I'll be back directly," the woman told him.

Marcus pulled up the collar on his jacket as the cool night air began to set in.   Several yards away the man Pete sent to follow Marcus watched from behind a building.   A while later the lady came back with a plate with two big rolls and a plate of beans with a cup of coffee.

"Thank you, ma'am, this sho' does look good.   I sho' do appreciate it," Marcus said.

"Well, when you get finished you go over to that pump and wash your dishes and leave them on the doorstep and get on out of here," the lady told him.

"Yes, ma'am, I sho' will," he replied.

"That'll be 45 cents."

Marcus paid the lady and sat down behind the restaurant and finished his dinner.

After Marcus finished his food he did as he was told and washed everything and placed them neatly on the back doorstep.   He walked back over to his horse and mounted up.   He rode out to the town's edge and found a small thicket of trees at the base of a hill.   The hill faced the north so he knew it would help block the wind.   He unsaddled his horse and rolled out his bedroll.   He lay down and had a good restful sleep.

The man that was sent to follow him went around town asking about Marcus, but no one knew who he was.   The lady at the restaurant said she had never seen him before.

"No, I ain't never seen him before, and he didn't cause no trouble.   After he paid me for the food, I came back and them dishes was washed and he was gone," she told him.

Late that night Pete's hired hand rode back out to the ranch and woke him up.   He said he followed Marcus and he didn't cause no kinda trouble.   He just rode into town, got something to eat then rode out of town and made camp.   "I asked around, ain't nobody ever seen or heard of him before."

"All right, all right, lad, thank you," Pete said.   He went back to bed and was awakened the next morning by the sound of Marcus knocking on his front door.

Pete answered the door, pulling a suspender strap over his left shoulder. "Ah, Mr. Smitty, wasn't it? Good morning."

"Good morning Mr. Pete, I done like you told me and came back this mornin'," Marcus said.   "I sho' do need that job, sir," he added.

"Yes, of course, the job," Pete said.   "I tell you what, it just so happens I could use a hand to help my cook.   He cooks for my guests and me but, he has a hard time getting food out to my hands in the field and the bunkhouse sometimes.   Your job will be to help him and make sure all of my cowboys are fed.   You will also rustle wood and wrangle horses."

"Yes, sir, yes, sir, I sho' can do that, don't you worry, Mr. Pete, I'll make you a hand for sho'," Marcus said.

Pete really did need some help for his chef, but he still wasn't completely sold on Marcus, or Smitty as he knows him.   Pete introduced Marcus to the chef and left them together.

"Howdy, sir, my name is Smitty, that's what folks call me."

"Well, Mr. Smitty, my name is Pierre Lavelle.   I am from New Orleans.   I am a classically trained French chef.   I used to be the head chef of the riverboat 'Charmer'.   Have you ever heard of it?"

"No, sir, I ain't never heard of it," Marcus answered.

"Of course you haven't, I don't know why I thought you would," Pierre said condescendingly.   "The Charmer was the biggest, finest riverboat anywhere to be found on the Mississippi.   I have served European royalty and American business titans as well as the highest elected officials of both the Confederacy and the Union."

"If you don't mind me askin', sir, why ain't you still there?   Why you cookin' on a ranch out here in Texas?" Marcus asked.

"Well, not that it is really any of your business, but I became a little too friendly with the young wife of the very hot tempered and completely unreasonable ship captain.   I decided a change of scenery would be in the best interest of everyone involved," Pierre told him.

"Yes sir, I guess I could see where that might be a problem," Marcus answered.   Pierre shot another condescending look at Marcus, then soon dismissed it.

Pierre told him what his responsibilities would be. He showed him where everything was and when the cowboys should be fed. He showed him a small room in the barn where he could stay. Pierre assured him that he had little patience for mistakes. Marcus assured him that he was a quick learner and he would make a hand.

The next few days went off without a hitch. Marcus did exactly as he was told and actually was making a fine hand. He made sure all the cowboys had plenty to eat. He would feed them at the bunkhouse and take a wagon out to a couple of the line shacks and make sure those cowboys had the supplies they needed. He would also work around the barn doing odds and ends.

Meanwhile, the men plotting to overthrow Pete O'Reilly went about their business. Each day one person would take turns riding past the live oak tree in front of Pete's ranch to see if the two rocks had been placed in the north fork of the tree. After a week or so Charley came riding back to Sam's ranch. As he got closer, Zeke met him in the yard.

"Well, did you see anything?" Zeke asked.

"Nah, nary a stone," Charley said dejectedly.

"I wonder what's goin' on out yonder," Zeke said.

"I don't know.   I hope he's doing all right," Charley said.

"Yeah, I been worried about this whole thing working since we let him ride off," Zeke said.

About that time Sam came out of the house to greet Charley.   "Charley boy! What's the good word?" Sam asked.

Charley shook his head and told him there were still no rocks in the tree. "Where's Chente and Mario?" Charley asked.

Sam said they were in the house finishing a letter they were about to mail back to Chente' s wife in Presidio.   She must have been worried sick, not having heard from her son or husband in a few weeks now.   Chente and Mario were definitely determined to stay with Sam and see this thing out. They would go home when Pete was dead or they were.

The next morning Mario said he would ride by the oak tree and check for the stones.   He needed to go to town anyway to post the letter he and his father had written.   He saddled up that morning after breakfast.   After sliding his rifle down in the scabbard and tying it off, he hopped up on his pony and told everyone he would be back late that afternoon.   He gave his horse a kick and they started down the road away from Sam's ranch.

A few hours later he rode past the old oak tree and noticed nothing had changed. Mario was upset. All this suspense and waiting was killing him. He wasn't bloodthirsty, not at all, he was just eager to get this thing going so they could get the revenge they were after and everyone could get on with their lives. He didn't make any kind of a scene around the ranch; he just kept on riding by, minding his own business headed for town.

A couple hours later he rode into town. As usual not much was going on, it was quiet and everyone was going on about their business. His first stop was the post office. He stopped in there and mailed the letter to his mother. He felt much better now knowing that in a couple of days she would be able to relax knowing that Mario and his dad were okay.

Mario had been in the saddle all morning and wasn't looking to jump right back in it, so he decided to eat lunch while he was in town and stretch his legs a little bit. He walked into the same little restaurant that Marcus had been in a week earlier. As he entered, there was a new dishwasher that noticed him walk in. The dishwasher looked over at the old lady who ran the place and asked her if they served Mexicans.

She replied, "Hell yes, we serve Mexicans. If we didn't in this part of Texas, we'd all starve to death!"

"Well, fine, you don't have to yell. I was just asking. I heard about that nigger that ate over here the other day!" The dishwasher answered. Mario overheard what the dishwasher was saying and that caught his attention.

"Well that was different," the owner said. "That was the first one I'd seen here since them army boys from Ft. Concho came in a year or so back. I can afford to have them boys eat out back."

The owner walked away from the dishwasher and came over to where Mario was sitting down. "Howdy," she said.

"Howdy," Mario answered.

"What can I get for you today?" she asked him.

"Just whatever your lunch special is and a beer," Mario said.

"We don't serve no beer in here, this is a Christian establishment," she snapped back. "Sorry, coffee will be fine then, ma'am," Mario answered.

"Well, we got beef stew with cornbread for lunch, will that suit ya?" She told him.

"Yes, ma'am, that will be fine." Mario thought this would be a good time to ask about Marcus.

"Did I hear you say you had some black trouble the other day?" Mario asked her.

"Nah, he weren't no trouble . . . just some runaway slave lookin' for a meal, panhandlin' round my back door."

"What happened?" Mario asked.

"Nothin' much, I fed him a plate out back, he paid me. I told him to wash his dishes and then get on down the road," the owner told him.

"Did he do it?" Mario asked.

"Yeah, come to think of it, after he ate I didn't hear nothin' else out of him. Huh, you know, if they'd all act like that they'd probably be a lot easier to tolerate, huh?"

"Yes, ma'am, I guess everyone just needs to know their place in this world!" Mario said in a sarcastic tone that she never picked up on.

"Well, son, we'll have yer food out directly, you just wait here," the lady told him.

Mario realized that was all the info he was going to be able to get out of her, so he just finished his meal after they brought it out. He paid his bill, thanked the lady and left. He hopped on his horse and started making his way back out to Sam's place. He passed the old oak tree one more time and there were still no rocks in the fork. Dejected, Mario spurred his horse again and rode back to the ranch.

Meanwhile, the next morning at Pete O'Reilly's ranch, Marcus was given the chore to cook a big barbecue for all the gunmen, excuse me, cowboys, that worked on the ranch to show how much Pete appreciated them. Marcus figured this would probably be as good a time as any to make his move.

Pierre told Marcus he was taking a couple of days off because he needed a break and second, he didn't do barbecue. He believed that was a black man's peasant food, and it was beneath his standards of cooking. Plus O'Reilly had made him do it once before and it turned out terrible, as he had no natural feel for it. Marcus had never cooked a cow before. He had barbecued more pigs than he could remember back in Alabama, so he figured this couldn't be much harder. He began to gather all the materials he would need. He also knew he would need an excuse to get out to the oak tree and put those stones in there so the boys could attack the next morning.

Marcus walked up to the door of the main house and knocked on the door. When Pete opened it Marcus put his hat in his hand and told him that he needed to make a trip to town to get a few things for the barbecue. Pete told him that was fine, go and get what he needed but hurry back.   He wanted to eat this food for lunch tomorrow, not dinner tomorrow night, knowing it would take several hours to make the barbecue right.

Marcus hurried out to the barn and saddled up his horse.   He was just about to put his foot in the stirrup when one of the cowhands walked in.

"Where in the hell are you going, boy?"   The man said.

"Oh, howdy there, sir," Marcus replied, a little bit startled.   "I gots to run into town and get some things for Mr. Pete's barbecue," Marcus said.

"Like what?   We got everything out here we need.   We run it that way so people don't have to be running off to town all the time," the man told him.

"Uhh, I need me some garlic cloves and black pepper," Marcus said.

"Is that all?   Hell, I got that out in the bunkhouse.   I used to help Pierre do a little cookin' before you ever showed up," the man said.

Marcus was startled but then he smiled and said, "You sho' right sir, I forgot all 'bout the ones we had out there in them cabinets. But, uhh, I gots to get me some fensical," Marcus said, throwing out the first word he could think of.

"Fensical?   What in the hell is that?" the man asked.

"Oh, you ain't never heard of no fensical?   It's a wild herb that grows all over Alabama.   I've heard tell that you can let it dry and it'll keep.   That way you can ship it to different parts of the country.   Yes, sir, you sho' gots to have you some or it just ain't barbecue.   Well, I gots to get going.   Mr. Pete done told me not to be wastin' no time," Marcus said as he finally mounted his horse and rode past the man.

Marcus hit a high lope just after leaving the barn.   He was scared to death; he hated lying and had never been any good at it.   The last thing he wanted to do was lose his nerve and not follow through with his end of the plan.

The cowboy in the barn still wasn't buying Marcus's story, so he decided to saddle up and follow him at a distance to see what he was really up to.   The cowboy took a short cut and was sitting behind a large rock outcropping and some cedar trees when he saw Marcus ride by the big oak tree.   He watched him dismount and pick up two rocks about the size of your palm.   He placed them in the tree then started back to his horse.   About that time the mysterious cowboy rode out from behind the rocks and confronted Marcus.

"Boy, what they hell do you think yer doin'?" the man asked.   Marcus was really scared now and he tried to lie the best he could.

"What? That? Naw, that's nothing, sir, it's just a little silly old superstition us black folk have. It supposed to be good luck to put two stones in a tree," Marcus told him with a nervous laugh.

"You know what it looks like to me boy? It looks a whole hell of a lot like you was leaving a signal or a sign for somebody," the man said.

"A sign? No sir, no sir, it ain't nothin' like that. No sir, not at all," Marcus answered.

"I tell you what, boy, how 'bout you and me take a little ride back to the ranch and you can tell Mr. O'Reilly about this silly superstition."

Marcus knew the game was over. The man slowly reached down for his gun, but Marcus knocked him to the ground with a crushing right hand. As the man lay on the ground seeing stars, Marcus reached for his knife on his hip and sliced the man's throat open. The cowboy gurgled and died instantly.

Marcus threw the man up on his horse and led him out into a thick patch of woods that no one ever rides down. He threw the man's body over a small cliff into a dry creek bed at the bottom. As for his horse, he unsaddled it to take the weight off and make it more comfortable. He couldn't release the horse and take a chance of it showing up at the ranch without a rider. That could spoil everything. He took the reins and tied the horse off good to a cedar limb. If he lived through the next couple of days, he would come back and release the horse, but right now he had to make sure it stayed put.

After he had disposed of the cowboy, Marcus made a flying trip into town so he wouldn't show back up at the ranch empty handed. When he got back he looked and the stones were already out of the tree so he knew that Zeke and the boys got the message. He noticed a blood spot on the ground where he had cut the cowboy. He quickly dismounted and wiped it up and tried to kick dirt over it, hoping no one had already noticed it.

When he arrived back at the ranch, Pete happened to be sitting on the porch. "Took you long enough, didn't it," he yelled in his thick Irish accent.

"Yes sir," Marcus answered. "But don't you worry none, Mr. Pete, this here's gonna be a barbecue you ain't never gonna forget."

Marcus did have a secret ingredient planned for the barbecue. It was a mixture of castor oil and gunpowder. He had never tried it before but his hope was that he could mix them together and the oil would coat the gunpowder, keeping it from exploding while the meat was cooking. Once it hit the stomach you would get the double trouble of a laxative churning your stomach with gunpowder mixing in your stomach acid. He wasn't sure what it would do exactly, but he knew it couldn't be good, and they certainly wouldn't be in any mood to get in a gunfight.

Marcus took the briskets he was preparing and sliced them open. He mixed the oil and gunpowder together and poured it almost like a paste on the meat and then closed the butterfly flap back up. After that, he seasoned the meat like you would anything else. He wrapped them in burlap sacks and placed them on a smoldering bed of coals to begin the long, slow process of cooking.

At the same time, back at the ranch, Chente came riding up. "He did it! He did it! He finally put the stones in the tree." Everyone came out of the house.

"Are you sure?" Zeke asked.

"Si, I am positive, I saw it with my own two eyes. That's not all, Señores, there was a spot of blood on the ground near there and two sets of fresh horse tracks leading off into the woods away from the ranch turn off."

"Damn, I wonder if Marcus was found out; I wonder if he is okay," Zeke asked.

"I think he is," Chente explained.

"Why do you say that?" Sam chimed in.

"Well, I know the tracks Marcus's horse makes when he rides it. Those same tracks come out of the woods and headed back towards the town. They are pretty fresh. I don't know, but my guess is somebody saw him there and there was a fight, maybe he hid the body so no one would find it," Chente said.

"Well we should go look for it," Charley added.

"Nah boy, I don't think that's a good idea," Sam said.

Chente added, "Sam is right. It would be too obvious to go that close to his ranch and snoop around. Besides, we really don't have the time to go over there, look around, and come back, even if we didn't get caught. I say we follow the plan as we discussed.

Zeke shook his head and said, "Yeah, Chente' s right, we best just stick to the plan."

"What do you reckon he's doing right now back at Pete's place?" Sam asked.

"I ain't got no idea," Zeke replied as he let out a long breath.

"Well, come on y'all, let's get back in the house and go over the plan one more time to make damn sure everybody's on the same page," Sam said.

Everybody went back into the house and sat down at the table. Sam pulled out a rough hand drawn map of the ranches. Since he knew this area better than anyone he was pretty much in charge of logistics.

"All right, we ain't got enough men to spare so we are gonna all have to split up. Zeke, you'll ride up directly to the house and try to draw Pete out. Make damn sure you already got a pistol in your hand; just keep it down by your saddle horn and out of sight.

All right, Charley, I hear you're a pretty good shot so you are going to be up on this ridge here. There is a little draw that comes off a hill on the northeast side of his ranch. Ride up that draw as far as you can. Tie your horse off and walk the rest of the way. I've seen it before and there is a rock table above his house that you can look right down on. You should be able to get some good shots down towards the house and barn.

Chente, you'll be on the opposite side. There is plenty of good tree cover, so you should be able to ride in fairly close and get a good look at the barn and the house. Me and Mario will ride up the back of his ranch from my ranch. If anybody spots us, I'll just say I'm looking for some cows that may have got out this way and I just hired this boy to come work for me. We'll do our damndest not to start any trouble back there but if it all goes south everybody's on their own. When we get to the back close enough to the house, me and Mario will spread out to try and cover more ground. Now if we all do make it and get into position, we'll basically have them surrounded, but there will be gaps big enough to drive a herd of cows through.

Zeke, you try and call Pete out. If you can get him out in front of you, go ahead and take the shot. If you drop him maybe his boys will realize they ain't gonna get paid no more and they'll just give up the fight. After you fire, get out of there, don't try and be no hero, 'cause we ain't giving out no medals. Find you some cover and wait for the fun to begin!"

Sam looked around and asked everyone if they understood what their job was. Everybody shook their head in agreement. This was it . . . there would be no turning back now.

Charley asked the one question no one else had thought of, "What time do we do all this tomorrow?"

Everybody kind of looked at each other. It was impossible to know the best time to attack since they had no way to communicate with Marcus.

"Think we ought to hit 'em at dawn?" Charley asked.

"Yeah, hit them when they are just waking up. They won't know what's going on," Mario said.

Sam scratched his old handlebar mustache and said, "I don't know, what do you think, Zeke?   Think we art to give him some more time?"   Zeke really didn't know what the best move would be.

"Chente, what time did you find them stones yesterday?" Zeke asked.

"I guess it was around 3 o'clock," Chente answered.

Zeke scratched the back of his head and said, "Damn, I just don't know.   If we attack at dawn and he ain't ready, we're gonna have a bloodbath on our hands.   But I reckon if we wait a bit and give him some more time, it wouldn't hurt nothing.   Even if he was ready for us at daybreak, a few more hours probably ain't gonna change nothing."

Sam asked, "Well, what do you figure he did to 'em?"

"I don't know.   What would you do if you wanted to take out a whole bunch of people by yourself at once?" Zeke answered.

"Poison!   That's it . . . poison!   Zeke, you remember when we got in that big fight in that creek in Virginia?   What was the only thing that kept us from all gettin' wiped out by them yanks?" Sam said.

"They all got sick from drinkin' out of that creek and couldn't fight.   The water had been poisoned upstream because that Yankee army hospital was throwing all them body parts and bandages in the creek, and it poisoned all the water downstream.   When we hit that Yankee outpost, they didn't stand a chance.   'Though we didn't know it at the time, they was three times the size of us, but they had come down so sick they couldn't hardly stand up, much less fight."

Chente added, "Marcus did say that a cook was one of the jobs he would ask for.   It makes sense.   If he poisoned them for breakfast or dinner, they would be in no shape to fight back.   That would definitely give us the upper hand."

Zeke finally decided, "Okay, here's what we're gonna do; we'll set up late in the morning, around 11 o'clock, and we'll sit there and watch 'em for a while. If he poisoned them at breakfast, they ain't going nowhere.   If he's gonna poison them at lunch, they ain't gonna want no part of a gunfight.   And if we're wrong on both counts, Lord, help us all!"

The Reckoning

The next morning the men all saddled up and began to make their way down to Pete O'Reilly's ranch. Mario and Sam were the first ones to pull off from the crowd because they were going to ride up the back of Sam's ranch and come in through the rear. Chente was the next one to pull off because he was going to hide out along the wood line behind the barn. Charley rode on past Zeke so he could take his position on that high ridge above the house. Zeke made his way along the road that led up to the main house.

This was it, there was no turning back. If Marcus had done his job, they might live through this, but nothing was guaranteed. If Marcus had not done his job, this was pretty much a suicide ride and all the men knew it. Each man had had his own taste of violence over the years. Zeke and Sam were both Civil War veterans. Chente had fought with his father from time to time over the years, protecting their ranch and their herds of horses. Charley and Mario were the newest to all the bloodshed. They had recently gotten a taste of it when they foolishly attacked Pete's ranch a few weeks back.

Zeke cautiously approached the ranch. His head swiveled back and forth, looking for any signs of trouble along the way. He got as close as he could without being seen from the road. He stopped his horse and began to look around to see if he could see Charley or Chente. They were each carrying small pocket mirrors to reflect the sun to let each other know they were in position. It turned out it was a cloudy overcast day so the mirrors were useless.

Zeke saw the ridge above the house where Charley was supposed to be. He could not see anything up there. He was hoping Charley was just being cautious not to give himself away. He looked the other direction back towards the barn. About thirty yards past the barn was the tree line, and he thought he could see someone or something posted over in that area but he was not sure. He was going to have to go on faith that it was in fact Chente. It was about 11:15 am when all this was taking place. Zeke decided to ride off into the wood line and wait about an hour until it was after 12 noon to see if anything had taken place.

An hour came and went; Zeke had not been noticed by anyone.   He looked at his pocket watch; it was now 12:20 pm.   He knew this was it.   He couldn't afford to put it off anymore.   He reached over and grabbed his rein from a nearby tree branch and put his foot in the stirrup.   He slung his leg over his horse and gave her a slight kick.   The horse started to make its way up to O'Reilly's front porch.   He kept looking around as he got closer but had no way of knowing if Charley, Chente, or anyone else could see him.   As he got up near the house he could see that a couple of big picnic tables had been set up with red and white checkered tablecloths.   He could smell some delicious barbecue cooking.   There were a bunch of cowboys sitting around the table.

It was an odd sight because nobody looked too happy.   Several men were doubled over in pain and some were seen running towards the outhouses. He even noticed a couple down on one knee holding their stomachs in great pain.   Zeke looked over where the pit was dug in the ground.   He noticed Marcus was over there and so was Pete O'Reilly.   O'Reilly was chewing him up one side and down the other.

"You stupid, ignorant Nigger!   What is wrong with you?   You told me you could cook!   Look around you.   Does this look like happy eaters?" Pete said in a deep, irate Irish accent.   About that time he raised his hand and slapped Marcus so hard that his hat spun off and he fell to one knee.   Marcus was furious.   His first instinct was to jump back up and kill O'Reilly, but he was trying to stay with the plan and give everyone a chance to be where they were supposed to be.

Pete raised his hand and clenched his fist.   He was about to unload on Marcus while he was still down on one knee.   About that time he heard a shout, "O'Reilly!"   Pete turned around and saw Zeke on his horse riding towards him.   Pete stopped what he was doing.   He started to walk towards the oncoming horse.   Pete knew something was up now.   He just didn't know what it was.

At that same time, Zeke hollered out, "Run Marcus!"   Zeke pulled the pistol he was carrying near the saddle horn and took one shot at O'Reilly.   He nicked him in the left shoulder.   Pete spun around and fell to one knee. Marcus got up as fast as he could and started running towards the house. Pete was about to try and return fire to Zeke but he had already turned his horse and started riding for cover.   O'Reilly changed his mind and went after Marcus, hoping to use him for a hostage.

Everyone heard the shot.   Charley opened up from the top of the hill and picked off two sick cowboys near the picnic tables.   Chente moved in from the wood line and fired from behind the barn.   He dropped one cowboy just as he left the outhouse and was pulling a suspender over his shoulder.   Sam and Mario were in position on the back of the ranch and they were holding steady in case any of the cowboys made a break for it that way.

Gunfire continued to ring out for the next few minutes. Smoke and dust was kicked up everywhere. All the cowboys who had been sick and vomiting gun powder and castor oil were now trying to focus on the men who were trying to kill them. Shots seemed to be ringing out in all directions.

Zeke had found some cover for himself behind a stack of rocks. He continued to fire into the crowd that was around the picnic tables. He was relieved to hear gunshots coming from the barn and ridge. He knew everyone must have gotten into their proper places before all the shooting started, but he still didn't know if they would make it out of this alive.

Everyone had sort of become stationary. Sporadic gunfire rang out from different places around the ranch. A few of the cowboys decided the only way to make it out alive was to try and run out the back way. Mario and Sam had slowly been working their way closer up the back side of the ranch after the shooting started. As a couple of them started to run out past the outhouse, they began to think they were home free, even though their stomachs were in excruciating pain. They ran as fast as they could while holding their stomachs with one hand.

They were both breathing hard as they neared the closest set of oak trees. All of the sudden Sam and Mario appeared from behind both trees and dropped each cowboy with one shot a piece. There was a splatter of blood and the boots of each man went up over their heads as they fell backwards.

After killing the first two cowboys that tried to run out, they decided to hold steady behind those oak trees. It was a good vantage point. They could see the entire back side of the ranch house, barn, pens and out buildings. They sat there and watched as shots continued to ring out.

Chente slowly tried to start closing in near the picnic tables. He worked along the edge of the barn wall, not to give himself away. Whenever he could set up for a good shot he would take one. The cowboys were clearly in no shape to fight. The pain in their stomachs was nearly debilitating and the natural human fear of being shot at was not helping matters either. Some of the men tried to low crawl to safer places. It was a combination of trying to stay low for safety reasons and physically not being able to lift themselves up to move very fast.

A couple of the cowboys managed to turn over a picnic table and began to return fire towards Chente at the barn. He was now pinned down a bit at the edge of the nearest round corral. They traded shots back and forth, two against one.

From up on the hill ridge, Charley could see that Chente was pinned down a bit so he tried to make his way farther over past the house and see if he could get a better shot at the men behind the picnic table. Charley knew he was giving up some protection by moving further down that ridge, but there was no way he was going to let his uncle or anyone else down. Finally, Charley made it to a place where he could see well enough to see the two men hiding behind the flipped picnic table. Charley rolled over on his side and began to reload his rifle. Once he had another round chambered he rolled back over and exposed himself to get a good shot at the other men.

After his first shot, Charley killed one of the men behind the table but the sound and smoke gave his new position away on the ridge. A cowboy who had made his way to the back of the house and was hiding saw him and returned fire up the hillside. The bullet shattered a larger piece of rock in front of Charley and it sent shards into his face cutting him below both eyes.

Charley dropped his rifle and covered his face with both hands, yelling in pain. At first, he thought maybe he had been killed. But as the moments passed he realized he was not dead. His face was bleeding pretty badly and it hurt like hell but he realized he was no worse for wear. Charley made his way back over to his horse and got his canteen and a rag out of his saddle bag. He washed the blood off his face the best he could and held pressure to stop bleeding so he could get back and get into the fight.

While all this firing continued Zeke had picked off a couple of exposed cowboys, but he was more worried about Marcus. Marcus had made his way into the house when the shooting began, but he knew O'Reilly had made his way in there too. While all of the shooting was going on outside, nothing had come from inside the house. Zeke figured O'Reilly was taking cover and using Marcus as a bargaining chip to get out of this thing alive.

Zeke tried to work his way up to the house as close as he could. His intention was to get inside the house but he would really have to expose himself and make a mad dash the last twenty yards or so to get up on the porch and inside the house. Zeke began to yell inside the house for O'Reilly to come out and fight. Pete finally responded with a couple of pot shots out the window back towards Zeke's general direction.

This back and forth went on for another ten minutes or so. Basically, Zeke and Pete were trading shots and shredding the front of Pete's house.

Once, Zeke yelled into the house, "Marcus, are you okay in there?"

He responded, "I'm okay." About the time he got the words "okay" out of his mouth, Zeke heard a blunt hit. It sounded like Pete had hit Marcus in the head with a butt stroke from his rifle.

Meanwhile, Mario and Sam had not seen anyone else making a run for the back of the ranch, so they decided to work their way in closer to help out everyone else. Once they were in good pistol range, they opened up on some of the cowboys who were lying on the ground firing aimlessly at anyone in shooting distance.

Finally, after a couple more minutes of sporadic gunfire, it seemed to get quiet. Soon everyone realized that O'Reilly's men were dead. Although most of them died from gunshot wounds a few of them actually died from the poison. The only blood on them was around their mouths where they had vomited large amounts of blood from the food.

All the men slowly closed in on the ranch house. The only sound anyone could hear was the sand and dirt crunching under the boots of the men moving in. All of the sudden the silence was shattered when Pete O'Reilly came bursting out of his front door. He kicked it wide open. In one hand he had Marcus by the collar of his shirt. In the other hand, he had a pistol to his head. Pete stood behind Marcus, using him for cover.

"That's far enough, stranger," Pete said as he stared down Zeke, wondering if he had ever met him before. "Who in the hell are you?"

Zeke stood up and faced Pete like a man. He responded, "My name is Ezequiel McDaniel and I'm here to put an end to all this thieving and killing."

While Pete and Zeke were introducing themselves, Charley, Chente, Sam, and Mario all made their way from around the back and sides of the house to the front. Each one of them had a gun trained on Pete.

O'Reilly caught a glimpse of all them out of his peripheral vision and said, "Well, I will be damned. I should have known you'd have something to do with this Sam Keller. It just goes to show you can't trust a kraut. And in true kraut fashion, I see you are still a coward. You can't fight your own battles; you had to recruit a nigger, some wetbacks, and a Scotsman. Keller... in all the world, did you really think I'd lose my land to you and a Scotsman? Do you have any idea how many Scots I buried in the old country?"

Sam replied, "I'd say none because you don't do your own dirty work. You hire these mercenaries you call cowboys to do all your killin' for ya. Now, this is over, Pete. You still got a chance to walk out of this thing alive. That's more of a chance than your boys ever had."

"No, I don't think so, Keller. If I gave myself up, you know as well as I that there would be a rope waiting at the Edwards County Courthouse. No sir, this ends here, today." Pete then turned his attention back to Zeke and said, "Is this your nigger? Does he belong to you?"

Zeke replied, "His name is Marcus, and he is a free man; he don't belong to nobody."

"Ah, but he is with you, isn't he? I never seen him around here before and I never seen you or these wetbacks or that other boy around here either. So I suppose you all came in together," Pete said.

"Yeah, Marcus works for me. What's that got to do with anything?" Zeke said.

"If you want to see him live, tell the others to put their guns on the ground and back away," Pete told him.

Zeke wasn't really great at hostage negotiations and he knew it. He and Pete stared each other down for a couple of minutes and finally, Zeke flinched first and said, "Okay, boys, do what he told ya."

Charley responded, "Uncle Zeke, you can't do it. He's gonna kill us all."

"Dammit boy, do like yer told. I'm giving the orders round here!" Zeke yelled back. "All y'all, dammit, do like he told you!" Zeke kept looking at Marcus; over all the time they had spent together he had really grown to respect Marcus and didn't want to see it end this way for him. Maybe their plan wasn't going to work after all but he didn't want to get Marcus killed over it; especially since he had survived so much already.

Everyone did what Zeke had told them to do. One by one you could hear the thud of a gun hitting the ground. Charley was the last to comply with his Uncle's command.

Finally, when Charley's pistol hit the Hill Country dirt, Pete looked over to Zeke and told him, "Okay, now you do the same." With a still stoic face, Zeke let his gun slip from his hand and hit the ground with the final thud.

Everyone was backing away from their guns the way they were told to when Zeke looked at Pete and said, "Okay, now what?"

"Now you die, Scotsman," Pete replied. As he said that he stepped out a bit from behind Marcus and pointed his gun directly at Zeke's head. Zeke stood there motionless. O'Reilly pulled the hammer back on his pistol, closed his left eye and began to squeeze the trigger. Zeke shut his eyes anticipating the shot.

All the sudden a huge shot rang out that echoed through the valley. Zeke opened his eyes and saw a huge splatter of blood from O'Reilly's head. The blood covered the side of Marcus's face as O'Reilly fell backward and hit the ground dead. Everyone except Marcus looked around to see where the shot had come from. Marcus was frozen stiff; he was trying to process in his mind what had just happened.

Zeke and everyone else turned and looked back towards the road leading into Pete's ranch.   All of the sudden Elizabeth stepped out from one side of a large oak tree and their young son Thomas stepped out from the other side. Thomas was holding a still smoking, carbine rifle.   They both came running up from behind the tree and tackled Zeke as they got to where he was standing.

"Lord have mercy, where did you two come from?" Zeke asked.

"We couldn't take it, Zeke.   We were not about to sit in that house and not know what happened here.   We figured if you died we wanted to die, too.   I already lost one son.   I couldn't bear the thought of losing another and a husband.   We just had to come and try to help," Elizabeth said.

"Whew, I sure am glad you did, Aunt Elizabeth, I sure am glad you did. Probably all of us would have left here feet first if you hadn't shown up," Charley told her.

"It wasn't just me, Charley, Thomas is the one who took the shot," she replied.

"Well I'll be damned, son.   I will be damned!   I sure am glad I taught you how to shoot boy," Zeke said with a sigh of relief.

"Me, too, Paw, it sure did come in handy, didn't it?" Thomas asked.   "Lord, it sure did, son, it sure did."

www.ingramcontent.com/pod-product-compliance
Lightning Source LLC
Chambersburg PA
CBHW021932170626
46807CB00007B/3067